Maylie AND THE MAZE

Maylie

AND THE
MAZE

"The world is a book and those who do not travel read only a page."
                                    - St. Augustine

That's one of Aunt Layla's favorite quotes. Now, I know why.

I've traveled to other countries and read a bunch of pages from the world's book with all the amazing people I met and every amazing thing I did.

Come with me, my friend, and I'll take you on a tour of the world!

Maylie
The Travel Girl

Tales of a Travel Girl series

Maylie's Luck of the Irish (Book Two)

Other books by M.L. Tarpley

Young Writer's Kit: A Guide for Young Writers
Tales of a Travel Girl coloring & activity book series

Maylie

AND THE

MAZE

TALES OF A TRAVEL GIRL

ENGLAND
BOOK ONE

M. L. TARPLEY
ART BY MONICA BRUENJES

INK MAP PRESS

Maylie and the Maze

© 2020 by Morgan Tarpley Smith

Published in Pollock, Louisiana, by Ink Map Press
www.inkmappress.com

Cover Design by Monica Bruenjes
Author photograph by Lynn Enterkin Photography

This is a work of fiction. Names, characters, places, and incidents either are the product of the author's imagination or are used fictitiously. Any resemblance to actual persons, living or dead, events, or locales is entirely coincidental.

Publisher's Cataloging-in-Publication Data

Names: Tarpley, M. L., pseud. | Smith, Morgan Tarpley, 1986 - . | Bruenjes, Monica, pseud. | Theiler, Monica, 1983 - .
Title: Maylie and the maze / M. L. Tarpley ; illustrated by Monica Bruenjes.
Description: Pollock, LA: Ink Map Press, 2020. | Series: Tales of a travel girl ; book 1. | Illustrated middle grade novel. | Audience: Ages 8-12. | Summary: Can a 10-year-old aspiring author overcome her overactive imagination and the most annoying twin brother ever to follow her dreams?
Identifiers: LCCN 2020915033 | ISBN 9781952928185 (hardcover) | ISBN 9781952928055 (paperback) | ISBN 9781952928048 (ebook)
Subjects: CYAC: Brothers and sisters–Fiction. | Creative writing–Fiction. | Friendship--Fiction. | England–Description and travel--Fiction. | BISAC: JUVENILE FICTION / Family / Siblings. | JUVENILE FICTION / People & Places / Europe. | JUVENILE FICTION / Travel.
Classification: LCC PZ7.1 T37 M3 2020 | DDC [Fic]--dc22
LC record available at https://lccn.loc.gov/2020915033

Printed in the United States of America
2020–First Edition

10 9 8 7 6 5 4 3 2 1

To my many nieces and nephews

May the world become your book & your dreams
take you places far beyond your imagination

Love, Gege

Table of Contents

"The moment you doubt whether you can fly, you cease forever to be able to do it."

J.M. Barrie *from* **"Peter Pan"**

Chapter One
Adventure Awaits!

I f only I had magic powers, this story would write itself.

Maylie Montes thumped her pen against the notebook and wished for the right words to zap to her brain. *Thwack. Thwack. Thwack.*

She read from her notebook again and groaned. "No, that's not right either." She must *really* be brain dead.

Her cat, Sparkles, uncurled from a silver ball of fur on the bed, narrowed her eyes, and sniffed the air. Maylie looked at her. "Do something to inspire me please. A backflip, anything?"

Sparkles held her gaze. Maylie watched as the cat lifted her head, yawned like a miniature lion, and fell back asleep.

"Thanks a lot," Maylie muttered. She was desperate for anything to jumpstart the story she'd tried to write for days, but she could never get past page one. How would she ever become a real author if she couldn't write a single story?

How did her favorite authors do it?

She ripped out the page, crushed it into a ball, and threw it on the floor. At that exact moment, a ball of paper smacked her in the forehead.

Maylie jerked her head up to see her twin  brother burst out in laughter, his blonde curls swishing. "Camden Lane, get out of here, or I'll tell Mom!"

Ugh. Like she needed any more distractions, especially not from her annoying brother. Maylie refocused and scribbled a line on a new page.

With another groan, she ripped it out too and crushed it extra small in her hand. Without looking, she flung it across the room.

"Got writer's block?"

Maylie looked up. Her aunt, Layla Rousseau, stood in the doorway looking at the sea of wadded paper littering the floor like a kiddie ball pit. Then, her aunt's focus went to Maylie's open suitcase with clothes and other items thrown around it. "I thought you were finishing packing."

"I am." Maylie sank to the floor and started shoving items inside her suitcase.

Her aunt bent to help her. "What's with all the paper?"

Maylie sighed. "I'm trying to write a story to submit to my favorite magazine. But–" She swept her hand out. "–as you can see, it's not going very well. I can't finish a story. I try and try, and I just can't. Something's wrong with me."

Her aunt smiled and put an arm around her shoulders. "May, there isn't anything wrong with you. Don't give up. You'll get there. Photography wasn't easy for me when I started either."

Maylie couldn't imagine it being hard for her.

Aunt Layla had an incredible job as a photographer for international travel magazines. She was always going on worldwide adventures.

And she was the reason Maylie, Camden, and their grandmother, Sue, who they called Grandma Suey, were going on a summer-long trip across Europe as her aunt covered photo assignments.

Maylie frowned. "No way. I'm sure you've always taken amazing photos." She pointed to her wall at a framed photo of African lions lying under a tree and another one of the shining Eiffel Tower. "You're famous!"

And it was true.

Her aunt *was* famous. Her photos from across the world were published in dozens of magazines. She'd even been interviewed on television.

Her aunt rolled her eyes. "Not always. I had to do the work, prove myself as one of the best, and take a lot of bad pictures first."

She sat back and studied Maylie. "You remind me of myself, May. You always have. There's a curiosity within you and a determination to follow your dreams. Keep at it. When I was serious about taking the kind of photos that people wanted to publish I traveled to Europe for the first time, and it helped inspire me. It could do the same for you."

Inspiration? That *was* what Maylie needed. And she had to prove herself and write not only a good story but the best one.

Maybe her aunt was right, and their trip would

somehow help her. She smiled. "Thanks, Aunt Layla."

"You're welcome." She bumped Maylie's arm. "Maybe we'll have a little fun along the way too."

Maylie hid a grimace. Her aunt's version of fun–mountain climbing, scuba diving, and chasing wild animals on a safari–didn't match hers. She shuddered thinking of hanging upside down off cliffs, getting bitten by a shark, or mauled by a lion. *No, thanks!*

Her aunt must have seen the fear on her face.

"I'm not taking you to the jungle or under the ocean, Maylie. It's only Europe. In fact–"

She stood and pointed to a spot on the huge world map stuck to the wall that she'd given Maylie last year on her ninth birthday. "–we're starting here–London, England. One of my favorite cities in the world. It's the first European city I ever visited. You're sure to find inspiration there too."

Maylie looked around her room at everything familiar and comfortable. She petted her cat. The

thought of leaving her best friend, Sarah, and even her little sister, Jayna, fluttered her insides.

"But I'm not brave like you, and I've never been anywhere. What if everything goes wrong?"

Her mind raced to its place of twirling, swirling what-if scenarios that her best friend liked to call her "*extreme zone.*"

London might not be the danger her aunt usually faced, but what if there was a plane crash, or she got hit by a bus, or their train was robbed?

She imagined being tied to a railroad track by an evil grinning man with a curled moustache like she'd seen in a cartoon. How would she survive that?

Maylie felt a hand on her shoulder and looked up to see her aunt's subtle smile. "It's going to be all right."

She helped Maylie up and with a grin said, "Finish up here, then let the adventure begin!"

After she left the room, Maylie faced her bed and the other notebook there with her packing list. She tapped off each item with a flick of the pen.

"Shirts, pants, jacket . . ." She couldn't forget anything. It wasn't like she could run home and grab a pair of sneakers if she needed them–not being that far away.

Thousands of miles from home . . .

Maylie swallowed the lump in her throat and petted Sparkles. She studied the giant world map on her wall.

Her eyes flitted from country to country like it was a connect-the-dots game. She would see some of those little colorful blobs very soon.

Maylie looked at her bookshelf. In particular, the shelf crammed with notebooks full of stories she'd never finished.

What about her dream of becoming an author? It was impossible if she couldn't finish writing anything.

Was there a chance the inspiration she needed was in Europe? In London? Or would she only meet her doom?

Chapter Two

The Anaconda Girl

Almost time to go."

Maylie heard her mom call from downstairs. She folded her arms and stared the notebooks down until a bright yellow one caught her attention. She grabbed it and shoved it into her suitcase.

And with the quick *zing!* of the zipper, she was packed and ready.

A loud wail like a weird police siren sounded from the hallway, and Maylie and Sparkles both jumped.

Her suitcase fell over with a thud, and Sparkles yowled in protest when another wail sounded. The cat's silver fur stood on end, and she rushed into Maylie's closet.

A blur of pigtails and flailing arms flew at Maylie from the doorway as missile quick her five-year-old sister, Jayna, clung to Maylie's waist for dear life. Her face pressed into Maylie's overalls as she squeezed her tighter.

Maylie gasped for breath and fought to untangle herself. "*Jayna. . .let go!*" The little girl's grip loosened. "Thank you. It's going to be okay."

"No, it's not," Jayna said in a muffled voice, her head still buried in the overalls. Then, she peered up with big blue eyes full of tears. Eyes exactly like Camden's, and she didn't want to think about him.

Besides the paper ball stunt earlier, he'd thrown her favorite shirt into the cat's litter. Eek! And it, uh, had to be thrown out.

Jayna wrapped her legs around Maylie until she hugged her like a tree trunk. Maylie stick-walked toward her bed and pulled on Jayna's arms enough to loosen her grip. "Girl, you are like an anaconda."

Jayna threw her head back and grinned while Maylie fully untangled herself and steered Jayna to sit on the bed. Jayna sniffed. Her head drooped, and pigtails wiggled. In a quiet voice, she said, "Do you *have* to go?"

Maylie sighed and put an arm around her

sister. "I'll be back before you know it." Maylie didn't exactly believe the words, but it was what her mom used to tell her when she was little.

"I'll miss you too much."

Maylie knelt in front of her sister. "I'll miss you too." She paused unsure what to say next. Then, the perfect plan came to mind. "But I need your help."

Jayna's chin lifted. Hope sparked in her eyes. "Really?"

Maylie smiled and pointed at Sparkles, who had left the closet and curled in a little silver ball on the rug. "I need *you* to take care of Sparkles. She'll miss me too, so you'll have to pet her and brush her and help Mom feed her. Can you do that?"

Jayna nodded and stooped to stroke the cat's shiny fur.

"You can help check the mail too because I'll send lots of postcards. *And* I'll buy you souvenirs."

Her eyes widened. "What's a *soo-vee-neer*?"

Maylie laughed. "It's a special present you buy when you travel. I'll buy you one from every single country."

"You will?" A smile lit her face.

"When I get back, you'll have a whole treasure chest of gifts. Won't that be great?"

"Yeah." Jayna's face brightened. She sailed into Maylie's arms. "You're the best!"

"*Not again*, anaconda," Maylie said with a laugh.

Jayna let her go and ran from the room yelling, "Mom, guess what!"

Maylie smiled and turned back to her suitcase. But before she reached it, an arm slipped around her from behind, and she jumped again.

"Jayna, if you don't stop that I'll–" She whirled around and stopped mid-sentence when she met the caramel eyes of her best friend, Sarah Carter.

"Oh. Not Jayna." Maylie smiled and hugged her. "Good. You're here." She pointed to the suitcase. "And I'm all packed."

Sarah smiled, and then it faltered.

Maylie took in the second gloomy expression of the hour. Sarah met her eyes. "I thought I was okay."

Maylie put a hand on Sarah's shoulder. "I know. But it's summer. School is *out.* No one should be sad right now."

"You'll be gone the *whole* summer, Maylie. I haven't let myself think about it until now."

Maylie pursed her lips. She didn't know what to say. She looked at Sarah and fought the tug of sadness and anticipation within her. She was about to embark on the adventure of a lifetime–and leave her best friend behind.

Sarah sighed. "But you're right. Nobody should be sad today." She squeezed Maylie's hand and smiled.

Maylie rested her hand on the suitcase handle. Sparkles stretched out her white front paws and yawned again. Maylie petted the silky gray back and forced away the sinking feeling in the pit of her stomach. She glanced around her room one more time.

Looking at Sarah, Maylie took a deep breath. *I will be brave and adventurous. I can do this.*

And something her aunt said still echoed in her mind.

She had to prove herself and be the best at writing. Work the hardest she had ever worked. Do better. Be better.

It was the only way to achieve her dream. And she desperately needed inspiration.

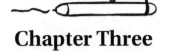

Chapter Three

Tools of Adventure

What's it like being ten? Do you feel any different?" Sarah asked as they walked from Maylie's room into the hallway. Maylie stopped pulling the suitcase and looked at Sarah.

Her friend's eyes searched hers as if turning ten the day before would have changed something in them. Maylie shrugged. "Not really, besides the two digits." She grinned. "I do think I should be more grown-up though. And this summer is the perfect time to–"

Whack! Her words stopped mid-sentence when a huge wad of paper slammed into her head.

Maylie's mouth dropped. Sarah gasped. Loud laughter rang out from down the hallway.

Her gaze met Camden's. His friend, Jin, was by his side, and they both held a mass of paper balls and laughed hysterically.

Maylie glared at Camden. Her mouth set in a deep scowl. She snatched a paper ball off the floor.

"Camden, I'm going to get you!" She jerked her hand back for a fast throw right at his head.

But, before she released it, her grip on the paper lessened. Her hand fell to her side. "We don't have time for these *childish* games," she said to Sarah.

Maylie thrust her chin into the air and walked away from her brother and his friend without so much as another glance in their direction. She tossed the ball over her shoulder.

Sarah smirked. "I can see your brother hasn't changed."

Maylie scoffed. Even though, she was only two minutes older than him sometimes it seemed like two years.

"I don't think he'll ever grow up. And he better not ruin our trip." She paused in walking. Her mind raced with possibilities.

But when Sarah touched her arm, she snapped out of it. "Fight the extreme zone, Maylie. Nothing will likely be as bad as your imagination."

Maylie shrugged. "True. I don't think he cares either way. He didn't really want to go on the trip anyway." She hadn't told Sarah that she hadn't wanted to go either, and she didn't mention it then. Instead, she took a deep breath, rolled the suitcase forward, and carried it downstairs with Sarah's help. She didn't look back.

Maylie and Sarah reached the foyer and watched Camden and Jin lug Camden's suitcase down with more than a bit of huffing and puffing. The monstrosity was bulging at its seams.

"Cam, what's in there?"

He rose to his full height, eye level with Maylie, and folded his arms over his chest. "None of *your* business."

Maylie narrowed her eyes and was about to make a snide remark when their parents and Jayna entered the room.

"Don't you two start," Mom said with a stern expression. "And if I hear you've been arguing you'll be on the first plane home. Do you understand?"

Maylie and Camden nodded but glared at each other from the corner of their eyes.

Their mom's attention turned to Camden's overstuffed luggage. "What is in that suitcase, Camden Lane?"

He shuffled to stand in front of it. "Everything I *need* for the trip."

"Let me be the judge of that." Mom waved her hand for him to move. He did so slowly. She opened the suitcase to reveal a large video game console, controllers, and a pile of games crammed on top of his clothes. She gathered it in her arms. "You *cannot* bring these."

"But, Mom, Jin will have all summer to practice. He'll be better than me." He looked at Jin for support, but he only shrugged.

"I'm sorry, honey, but you're only allowed to bring a handheld game console."

His face fell even more. "But Jayna broke it."

"Oh, that's true, isn't it?" Mom's frown flipped to a smile. She glanced at their dad, who held up a small red backpack. "I think we can fix that."

He handed it to Camden, who unzipped it in a fury and yelled, "Woo-hoo!" He shoved a notebook, drawing pad, pens, and pencils to the floor, and carefully removed a brand-new handheld console and two games. "Thanks!" He jumped up and hugged them.

Maylie hadn't seen her brother that excited in a long time, and it made her smile before she

24

remembered she was mad at him.

Mom turned her attention to Maylie. "Do you have everything you need?" she asked, staring at Maylie's non-bulging suitcase.

"I think so. I rechecked our list."

"Good girl. But I do think you're missing something."

Maylie's eyebrows drew together.

Her dad held up a brown messenger bag. "We thought the adventurer might need a special travel kit," he said with a grin.

Maylie's mouth fell open. Her fingers glided over the bag's soft fabric. She opened it–a unicorn notebook, drawing pad and all were there too but also a tiny stuffed cat resembling Sparkles and the new digital camera she'd wanted forever.

"*Muchas gracias, Tata!*" she exclaimed in Spanish, running into her dad's arms.

"*Mucho gusto, mi hija,*" he replied and kissed the top of her head. "We thought you'd need a way to document your trip whether writing, drawing,

or photography."

She and Sarah poured over the contents of her new bag while Mom added more clothing to Camden's suitcase, and then they loaded up for the airport.

Maylie and Sarah spent most of the ride trying out her new camera–zooming in and out at each other and the window. When the car stopped at a traffic light, Maylie zoomed in ahead of them through the windshield and spotted a series of brightly colored tubes high in the air.

The car lurched forward, and Maylie lost her view.

"I thought the water park was closed today," Mom said. "I see cars there."

Maylie and Sarah exchanged glances and frowned.

"It is," Maylie said in a low voice. "Jasmine Randolph's parents let her have a private party for friends when it's closed."

It was a *very* well-known fact that the Randolphs owned the super-popular waterpark, a favorite summer hangout for kids at their school–and the reason Jasmine had a lot of friends.

Dozens of multi-color slides snaked across the place, and a long, winding lazy river ran around them filled with floating tubes.

"Oh, that's nice."

"Sure, Mom." But it wasn't nice to Maylie at all. She and Sarah had never been invited. And

Jasmine made sure they knew it, even one time handing them a paper that read–NOT INVITED.

Maylie's head drooped. Sarah squeezed her hand. She hadn't forgotten what happened either. Maylie sighed.

Camden called out, "Look! There's the Super Sonic Snake, the new star attraction." Maylie peeked up at the huge black twisted slide as a guy was flung out of its tube into a huge pool of water.

"Whoa! You fly on that thing," Jin said. "I heard it's mostly in the dark. Uncle Cho is taking me next week. I'll be sure to tell you all about it."

"I'm going to miss everything," Camden whined.

Maylie couldn't believe her ears. "Really, Cam? A waterslide over Europe." He didn't care about the trip, which gave her more reason to think he might mess it up to come home.

Europe was where she'd find the inspiration she needed, and no one was going to stand in her way.

He shrugged and rolled his eyes.

Sarah leaned over and whispered, "Yeah, what's his deal? Your trip will make the water park look like a kiddie pool."

Maylie snorted with laughter, and Sarah stifled a giggle. Camden stared at them. "And, even better, Jasmine's eyes are going to bug out of her head when she finds out where you've been all summer."

The car stopped at a traffic light right outside the park. Maylie could see dozens of their classmates rushing around in swimsuits. "Yeah, I'd like to see her face when–"

Then, she saw him. *Alex Simmons*. The boy she'd had a crush on since first grade. And he was talking to Jasmine.

Maylie felt like she'd been slammed in the chest. She grabbed her camera and zoomed in. Jasmine tilted her head and smiled at him. She pointed to something across the park and leaned in to say something.

He turned and gave a high five to his best friend, Jackson. Then, the car lurched onward, and they were gone.

Next year at school will be different.

Maylie released a quiet breath and welcomed the thousands and thousands of miles that would soon separate her from everything she knew.

Chapter Four

Up, Up, and Away!

"Promise you'll take lots of pictures. I want to see *everything*," Sarah said after hugging Maylie for the third time. "And text me as soon as you can."

"Of course, I will!" Maylie replied, and then final hugs were given to everyone. She joined her brother, aunt, and grandma in the security line.

After removing her shoes and walking through the sensor behind Aunt Layla, she turned back and waved one more time before Aunt Layla urged them toward the boarding gate.

Now, it was time to be brave.

Maylie's fingers gripped the bag's strap until her knuckles shone white.

She walked down a long tunnel until she arrived at the plane's open door. A uniformed woman greeted Aunt Layla by name. She smiled at Maylie and directed her to enter.

The walking space was cramped, and Maylie was careful not to hit anyone with her bag as she passed them. Her aunt ducked left behind a wall, and Maylie had a full view of the plane.

Rows and rows and rows of seats stretched before her. People shoved bags into overhead compartments. Two seats in a long row ran along each side of the plane with three seats in the middle row.

Maylie spotted her aunt and clambered over. She took the seat on the side between the window and Aunt Layla. Camden and Grandma Suey sat behind them. Maylie distracted her nerves by watching the busy airport world outside the small oval window.

Men and women wearing vests walked around outside and some drove golf cart-like vehicles pulling carts piled high with luggage. She squinted to see if she could spot her blue suitcase with the purple ribbon on the handle.

She turned from the window to watch Aunt Layla re-arrange a bag in the overhead bin and push her shoulder-length red hair off her face.

It flipped up a bit at the ends and always look-ed a bit messy, but it fit her aunt's small build, like Grandma Suey's and her mom's, and gave her a youthful appearance, kind of what Maylie imagined a fairy or sprite from a story might look like in real life wearing jeans and a T-shirt.

Her aunt tucked a book into the seat pocket, and then her eyes met Maylie's with their usual sparkle. Maylie quickly looked away.

"Are you okay?" her aunt asked in a gentle voice.

Maylie shrugged and bit her lip. She gave a sideways glance and saw her aunt's expression soften.

"It's okay to be scared, May."

She met her aunt's eyes. "I'm not *scared.*"

Aunt Layla pointed to the bag clutched to Maylie's chest. "Why are you suffocating your bag then?"

She loosened her grip on the bag. "Okay, maybe I am a *little* nervous."

Her aunt nodded. "It's okay to be a little scared. I was on my first flight, and I was ten years older than you."

"Really?" Maylie couldn't imagine her aunt being afraid of anything. She traveled all around

the world, taking pictures of lava-spewing volcanos, roaring lions, and killer whales.

How could *she* be scared?

"Yes, but I discovered something. Doing new things may be scary, but they are some of the most memorable experiences." She gave Maylie's shoulder a squeeze. "So, don't worry."

Maylie's chest didn't feel as tight, and she only reached out for her aunt's hand when the plane roared down the runway and soared into the sky.

Afterward, they enjoyed a little tray of yummy lasagna for dinner, and she watched an in-flight movie on the tiny TV screen on the seatback while her aunt worked on her laptop.

Maylie took out the new unicorn notebook and tried to write something, but, instead, she stared at the first blank page for what seemed like an hour.

Nothing would come. She had no idea what to write. The page stayed blank.

"Having trouble?" Aunt Layla asked, looking up from her computer.

Maylie's frustration must have been etched on her face. "I'm trying to write a story, but I can't." She let her pen fall onto the tray with a *clack!* "How will I ever be an author if I can't write?"

Aunt Layla placed the pen back in Maylie's hand. "Don't be so hard on yourself. You'll learn how–in fact, I'm sure of it."

Her aunt's grin encouraged her but also sparked her curiosity. *What made her so sure?*

Before she could ask, Aunt Layla spoke up again. "Oh, I almost forgot to give you these."

She handed Maylie a copy of *Peter Pan* and a thin book with England sprawled across the front in large letters over a photo of a huge castle.

"The first is because *Peter Pan* is one of my favorite stories, and the book is partially set in our first stop–London. And this travel guidebook will tell you all about this country."

"Thank you!" Maylie brushed her fingers over the *Peter Pan* cover and flipped through the guidebook with photographs of more castles, huge houses, knight's armor, and a giant sort of Ferris wheel.

She spent the next hour reading the guidebook and doodling clouds and airplanes. The lights dimmed.

Aunt Layla put away her computer. "May, you

better get some sleep, or you'll be a zombie when we get there."

Her aunt winked and closed her eyes.

Zombies?! Travel makes you a zombie!

Maylie didn't chance it. She quickly put her things away and went to sleep. She certainly didn't want to be a zombie.

Hey family!

The plane ride was great! I'm not a zombie! I just got really tired. Aunt Layla said since it's 4 p.m. here it's 10 a.m. there. My body has to change time. Wow. London is amazing! At the British Museum, we saw statues and artwork from all over the world. We saw the royal jewels at the Tower of London. Some were as big as my fist. Cam's favorite part was the spot where people got beheaded. Ewww! I like riding the underground train called the Tube. I hope you are doing well. Pet Sparkles for me!

Love,
The Travel Girl

COUNTRY PROFILE

NAME: ENGLAND

CAPITAL: LONDON

POPULATION: OVER 54 MILLION PEOPLE

SIZE COMPARED TO U.S.: SLIGHTLY SMALLER THAN THE STATE OF ALABAMA

LANGUAGE: ENGLISH

CURRENCY: POUND STERLING

SOME WORDS TO KNOW:
TRAINERS — SNEAKERS
JUMPER — SWEATER
W.C. (OR LOO) — BATHROOM

FACTS:

- COMPARED TO THE U.S., PEOPLE DRIVE ON THE OTHER SIDE OF THE CAR AND THE ROAD.

- THERE ISN'T A PRESIDENT, BUT A PRIME MINISTER AND A KING OR QUEEN KNOWN AS A MONARCH.

- ENGLAND IS PART OF THE UNITED KINGDOM WHICH INCLUDES THE COUNTRIES OF SCOTLAND, WALES AND NORTHERN IRELAND.

- THE U.S. BECAME A NATION AFTER GAINING INDEPENDENCE FROM ENGLAND.

Chapter Five

So Not the Fair

Why did I do this? Higher than a 44-story building off the ground, Maylie, Camden, and Grandma Suey stood inside a glass pod of one of the world's largest observation wheels–the London Eye.

Maylie held tight to the railing. She forced herself not to look down into the murky river *far* below. But not looking didn't change the facts.

Deep breathe, Maylie. Remember what Sarah said. Resist the extreme zone.

"Look, Maylie!" Camden called from behind her. She turned to see him jumping up and down as hard as he could. "If I jump hard enough, we might fall into the Thames River!"

"Stop it, Cam! That's not true."

Even so, Maylie squeezed her eyes shut. Her breaths sped up, and her grip tightened on the railing until her fingers hurt.

Falling from this height, their pod would sink deep into the water or even worse crash to the concrete. . .or their entire pod could be snatched from the sky by a massive fire-breathing dragon and carried off to its faraway lair never to be seen again.

"Leave your sister alone." Maylie looked at Grandma Suey, who lightly gripped Camden's shoulder. "If you keep this up, we won't go to Harrod's for lunch."

He straightened.

"Now, come with me and enjoy this view."

Grandma Suey guided him away from Maylie,

who snapped photos to keep her mind from the possibility of plunging hundreds of feet. She heard Grandma Suey add, "And this river's name is pronounced *tims.*"

Camden had begged to ride it, and Maylie reluctantly agreed. He seemed to forget the nice things she did for him and always did his best to aggravate her–his favorite pastime.

Maylie focused her camera on the massive building of Parliament, England's government headquarters, across from them and the famous clock tower, Big Ben–the same one in the movie where Peter Pan and Wendy flew past going to Neverland.

She took out her England guidebook and saw a photograph of the exact view in front of her. On the page, she discovered that the tower wasn't "Big Ben" after all, but it was the name of the bell inside the tower.

Her attention wandered left to their neighboring pod. Through the glass, she saw people dressed in business suits holding drinks and plates of food.

A party in a pod?

She stifled a giggle and looked over her shoulder at her brother. "Cam, look over there," she said, pointing at the people. "It's an Eye-pod party. Get it!"

Camden howled with laughter, and Maylie was glad they were the only ones in their pod. He kept laughing until he was leaning on Grandma Suey.

"What's so funny?" Grandma Suey asked with a puzzled look on her face.

Maylie watched her brother, who wiped a hand over his eyes. "It's nothing, Grandma Suey. Just a joke."

Maybe if Maylie kept Camden laughing as much as possible he wouldn't cause problems.

45

She wasn't sure what happened between them. They went from best friends to barely tolerating each other.

Maylie was sure of one thing: his behavior would *not* ruin her trip.

The past few days in London had been unbelievable. And it was only week one. There was so much to see and do, and Maylie watched everywhere for a source of inspiration.

She breathed a sigh of relief as their "Eye-pod" touched back down, and they exited. She wanted to kiss the ground, but there was no time for that.

Grandma Suey kept a tight and busy schedule, which meant their tour bus pulled up precisely when they reached the pick-up spot.

The bus ride was a much-needed break for Maylie's feet. Grandma Suey wasn't an old gray-haired lady without energy. She buzzed around like a bee flitting from flower to flower. Maylie grew tired only watching her. They had probably walked a billion steps that day, but Grandma Suey was still going strong.

Maylie hopped on the bus and showed her pass to Mr. Johnson, the driver, who tipped his hat like a *proper* gentleman as Grandma Suey said.

Maylie smiled. He had been their bus driver off and on for several days. He was nice but had a strange accent.

When she'd asked him about it he'd told her he spoke *Cockney* and said things like *shant* instead of *shouldn't*.

"Goin' atop again, miss?" he asked, his teeth gleaming white against his dark skin.

"Yes, I am. And I'll make sure all is well, sir."

"See you do that, love. Run along now."

Maylie saluted and scrambled up the bus staircase. Yes, the bus had stairs.

At the top, she stepped into the open seating of the double decker bus. There was no roof or windows though the layout was identical to downstairs. Grandma Suey and Camden came up right behind her.

With the wind whipping her hair, she felt like she might shoot toward the sky on a great gust past the clock tower like Peter and Wendy and straight on to Neverland.

Chapter Six
Havoc at Harrod's

Parliament zoomed past, and the bus careened through streets and around many buildings that Grandma Suey pointed out were much older than the U.S.

This special tourist bus stopped at many places around London like Buckingham Palace, the official home of the United Kingdom's monarch.

Earlier that day, Maylie had taken a photo of it through the huge golden gates. She'd tried her best to get a close-up photo of a palace guard who wore a red uniform and a tall black furry hat.

The bus drove on past fountains with statues, fancy apartment buildings, and hundreds of pedestrians crossing streets and following the maze of sidewalks.

Grandma Suey leaned over to Maylie. "Next stop is us."

Maylie nodded, and they made their way downstairs. Their stop arrived. Maylie stepped off and waved to Mr. Johnson. "Goodbye, Mr. Johnson. Have a good day!"

"Cheerio, love! You do the same now."

Maylie, Camden, and Grandma Suey joined the crowd along the sidewalk. Maylie took her place by Camden in front of Grandma, so she could keep an eye on them and make sure they didn't get lost.

Soon, they stood under the dark green awning of the world famous Harrod's Department Store. Grandma Suey and Maylie admired a big display window nearby filled with sparkling necklaces and rings. Then, they turned to see Camden rushing for the entrance through glass double doors.

He collided with a lady coming out. She sailed forward onto the sidewalk and teetered on her very high heels.

Grandma Suey and Maylie's mouths dropped.

The lady balanced herself and smoothed down her slim-fitting yellow dress and the curls piled on top of her head. She whirled around to face Grandma Suey. "I have never! Control that little twit!"

Mouths still gaping, Grandma Suey and Maylie watched the woman turn on her heels.

"Tourists!" she exclaimed and marched away with her nose in the air.

Meanwhile, Camden disappeared zippity quick inside the store, and Grandma Suey followed him like a speeding bullet.

When Maylie tiptoed inside the building Grandma Suey had grabbed him by his shirt collar

and hauled him across the lobby.

Maylie hung back a few feet while her brother received an animated lecture. Grandma Suey's finger wagged in a fury in his face.

After a few minutes, she straightened and walked toward Maylie. "Okay, let's get some lunch."

Camden didn't say a word.

Maylie leaned over and whispered, "What did she use to threaten you?"

His eyes downcast, he replied, "She's taking a game for a few days and another one if I pull another stunt."

"Oh . . ." His games were important to him.

"I have to say losing a game was worth it if you'd seen that lady's face. She was so mad I thought the curls would explode off her head."

Camden laughed until Grandma Suey shot him a look over her shoulder.

In a quiet voice, he said, "I didn't mean to." He shrugged with a sheepish grin. "I couldn't help myself. My hungry stomach made me do it."

Maylie grinned. "You better keep your stomach in line, or you'll lose all your games. And–"

Her words skidded to a stop as they entered the open doorway. The food hall was as big as a football field!

Delicious aromas wafted through the air. Maylie's mouth watered.

A loud rumble erupted from Camden's stomach. She met his eyes, and they burst out in laughter. Then, she said, "Let's feed that."

Chapter Seven

A Promise Kept

Great googly woogly! Massive glass cases lined the long room and were tucked in the middle too with more dishes of food in them than Maylie had ever seen.

Workers in straw flat-topped hats, white shirts, and green aprons talked to customers across the dozens of counters or scooped up food from dishes.

Camden whistled and patted his stomach. "Where do I start?"

Maylie shuffled toward the nearest counter. All sorts of colorful pastries sat in layers behind the glass along with rows of thickly frosted cupcakes as big as her face. She felt a light tug on her arm.

"No dessert first," Grandma Suey said with a smile. She steered them over to the case of more pasta than Maylie's eyes could take in at once.

"Excuse me, sir," Grandma Suey called out to a worker behind the counter.

He stopped. "Yes, madam. May I help you?" he asked in a high-pitched proper voice.

"How do we go about ordering?"

"Ah, yes. Take notice of the small machines above each counter." He pointed to one nearby where a woman was removing a ticket. "Take a number and join the queue at that precise counter. Your number shall be called, and then you tell the server which dishes you would like and when to stop filling the container."

"I see," Grandma Suey said, glancing at the ticket machine. "Thank you." He gave a slight nod and resumed his work.

"I'm heading for the pizza," Camden said, eagerly rubbing his hands together. "Catch ya later."

"Oh no, you don't," Grandma Suey countered and placed a hand on his arm. "You will both stay right here with me, and we'll make the rounds for what you want." To enforce her point, she trod over to the nearest machine and grabbed a number.

The food hall ordering took a while until Maylie's stomach growled like an angry bear.

Their food filled six clear rectangular containers, the size of bricks, all stacked up inside tall green plastic bags.

"It's kind of like a Lego tower if you think about it," Camden said, staring down into a bag. He grinned. "I'll take edible Legos over regular ones any day."

Maylie grinned. "Me too!"

"I think it's dessert time now," Grandma Suey said.

Maylie searched out the giant blue cupcake calling to her.

Maylie swung her green bag at her side while she, Grandma Suey, and Camden walked through a huge and beautiful park that was near Kensington Palace, which was somewhere close by, but even as Maylie looked all around she hadn't spotted it.

A wide stream, or maybe it was a pond, Maylie thought, ran along beside her. She peered down over the black metal fence to see ducks gliding over the clear water filled with dancing green gras-

58

ses below its surface. She was trailing her fingers along the fence and watching a cute baby duck chase its mother when she collided with someone. She jumped back in fright until she looked up into the laughing eyes of her aunt.

"You're here." She threw her arms around Aunt Layla. "But I thought you had magazine meetings all day?"

"They could do without me for a little while," she said with a smile.

Camden came over and opened his bag. "Look at all my food Legos."

Aunt Layla laughed and peeked inside. Her eyes widened. "You sure you can eat all that, Camden?"

He raised his eyebrows and blurted out, "Does England have a monarch?" which sent Aunt Layla, Maylie, and Grandma Suey roaring with laughter.

Regaining composure, Aunt Layla looked at Grandma Suey. "You have Legos for me?" She was handed a bag.

Aunt Layla glanced back at Maylie and Camden. "Let's eat over here. I've got just the place." She led them a little farther ahead the path until to their right the trees gave way to a semi-circular opening with a tall statue promptly displayed at its center.

Maylie gasped. *Was that who she thought it was?*

She rushed over to get a better look. Yes!

"Peter Pan," she said, her voice coming out in a whisper.

Aunt Layla headed through the gate toward the statue. "Yes, it's 'The Boy Who Never Grew Up' himself. I thought you might like to see it."

Maylie and Camden followed behind until they all stood at its base and looked up at a bronze Peter Pan playing a long pipe that must be a flute, Maylie thought, with fairies, rabbits, and other creatures frozen in a swirl around his feet.

"*Hmm . . .*"

Maylie looked over at her brother. His head

tilted to the side as he studied the statue. "What is it, Cam?"

"I totally get not wanting to grow up, but I wouldn't want to stay a 10-year-old. I'm thinking maybe I'd stop at 17." He shrugged. "I mean I gotta learn to drive if I'm going to own the fastest sports cars in the world."

Maylie rolled her eyes. "Whatever, Cam. So, you wouldn't want to be a Lost Boy? No school, no parents, and live on an island?"

"That doesn't sound too bad," Camden said with a smirk until Grandma Suey's raised eyebrows wiped it right off his mouth. He threw a hand up. "Okay, okay, just no school would be fine. Let's eat. I'm starving."

Maylie and Aunt Layla exchanged amused looks, and they all sat on the raised platform under the statue and ate their lunch. Maylie's attention switched from the statue to the ducks in the river as she finished her pasta.

Did she want to grow up?

She looked at Aunt Layla, who traveled the world, did a job she loved, and went on adventures all the time. Yeah, she did. Until then, she would have to settle for acting more grown up.

Maylie licked icing off her fingers and bit her lip to hide a smile. Maybe she didn't want to grow up too quickly, she thought, as she savored every bite of the giant blue cupcake.

With a mouthful of green cupcake, Camden mumbled something she couldn't understand.

"Don't speak with your mouth full, Cam," Maylie said with a glare that rivaled their mom. "What did you say?"

He gulped down the huge bite. "Where are we going now?"

Grandma Suey patted her mouth with a napkin and then used one on Camden's green-streaked cheek.

"Yes, Grandma Suey, what's next?" Maylie said, curious as to her silence.

Grandma exchanged a glance with Aunt Layla

before she said, "The next stop is the British Library."

"For real." Maylie squealed and clasped her hands together. "I bet they have millions and millions of books."

"Oh, great," Camden muttered. "She's going to burst with excitement."

Aunt Layla shook her head at Camden and met Maylie's gaze. "That's not all. I've signed you both up for a Young Author's writing class."

Maylie yelped and pumped a fist into the air. Camden groaned. But Maylie didn't care. She danced around Peter Pan.

I'm going to learn to write!

Chapter Eight
Kindred Spirits

I'll be back after afternoon tea." Grandma Suey adjusted her purse on her shoulder. "You two behave and have fun."

"Do I have to stay?" Camden asked in a whiny voice. "This stuff is what Maylie likes. *Not* me."

"I know but give it a chance. You may learn something. Besides, there's a special activity coming up for you soon." She patted Camden's shoulder and then went out the door.

"It's time I get to do something I want," Camden said, crossing his arms and glaring at Maylie. "It's not fair. You always get what you want."

Maylie frowned and prepared to argue, but he stomped away and plopped into a chair at an empty corner table. He did not look at her.

I don't get everything I want.

Maylie marched to the room's front center table. She busied herself with preparing for the class, arranging her new notebook and a pen.

"Is that a unicorn on your notebook?" A soft British voice piped up from behind Maylie. She turned and met nearly face-to-face with a smiling girl who had long straight shiny black hair and skin like caramel.

The girl's large golden eyes twinkled behind slim rectangular glasses, and Maylie automatically smiled back and said, "Hi."

The girl squinted at Maylie and pushed her glasses up. "Is this seat taken?" She pointed to the

empty chair.

Maylie shook her head.

"That's brill. Cheers," the girl said and took it.

Maylie's eyebrows drew together. "What?"

"Oh . . . I suppose I should explain to a Yank, ey?" she said with a hint of a thicker British accent. "I'm Rana, Rana Peterson." Maylie introduced herself, and Rana continued, "'Brill' is short for 'brilliant,' and cheers is how we say, 'thank you'."

"I see," Maylie said and studied Rana intently.

Glancing at her notebook, she remembered to

answer Rana's question. "Yes, this is a unicorn. Do you like horses?"

Rana's eyes lit up. "Oh, yes. I love them. I've ridden in the countryside a few times."

"I do too. My brother and I ride horses with our cousins."

"Smashing," Rana said, and Maylie assumed it was a good thing. "Is your brother here?"

Maylie nodded and pointed at the back table. "The boy in the green shirt. The one with folded arms and the big frown like his pants are too tight."

Rana burst out with a blast of laughter, which turned into a fit of giggles.

Maylie stared at her. *What had she said?*

"I–I'm sorry," Rana said and struggled to catch her breath. "Here, pants are what you call 'underwear.' So, you said his underwear are too tight."

Maylie looked at her brother and snickered behind her hand. Camden glared at her.

"He's more than my brother unfortunately. He's my twin."

"Twin?" Rana exclaimed. She glanced at Camden and then at Maylie. "How interesting. You don't resemble him at all."

"We get that a lot." They were, in fact, polar opposites–Cam with blonde curly hair, blue eyes, and fair skin and she with brown wavy hair, brown eyes, and olive skin. "He looks like our mom, and I look like our dad, who was born in Costa Rica."

"Oh, wow. I believe that's in Central America, correct?"

Maylie raised her eyebrows. "Yes, but most kids don't know that. You must be very smart."

Rana shrugged. "I've always liked geography." She glanced to the back of the room again. "It seems your brother has some other gloomy mates." She nodded toward a few other frowning kids. "My older brother included. He's on the left in the red shirt. They look utterly miserable."

"Yeah, my mom says, 'misery loves company.' So, they can just be miserable together. But I won't let it bother me. I came here to write."

"So, did I." Rana took out a notebook with a brown cat on it. Maylie thought about Sparkles. *I hope Mom and Jayna don't forget to scratch her ears or throw her mouse.*

"I have a cat," Maylie said.

"Really? So, do I. In fact, Lily resembles this cat." She pointed to her notebook. "That's why I bought it."

Maylie grinned. "No way." She shuffled around in her messenger bag until her fingers slid across fur. She drew out the little stuffed cat and held it out to Rana. "This looks just like my cat,

70

Sparkles."

"How cute! May I hold it?"

Maylie placed it in Rana's outstretched hand. She stroked the silky silver fur before handing it back to Maylie. "My mom and dad gave her to me before I left home. In case, I get homesick."

"When did you leave?"

"Three days ago," Maylie said with a slight smile.

Rana matched it. "Not homesick yet, are you?"

"Not yet. I haven't had time to be. Everything has been so exciting. This is my first trip anywhere."

"You're certainly chuffed to bits. I would be. I've never been across the Pond myself."

Maylie tilted her head. "The pond?"

Rana touched her forehead. "Sorry. The *Pond* is what we Brits call the Atlantic Ocean." She shrugged. "Though, I'm not sure why."

Maylie grinned. "So, you are from here?"

"England, yes. London, no. I live an hour away

by train in Kent. Near a castle."

Maylie's eyebrows rose. "Wow. A real castle?"

"Yes, we have quite a few of those around."

"It's hard to believe. We don't have anything like that at home."

Maylie imagined a castle in her town by her favorite pizza place. It certainly didn't fit, but the idea of pizza being delivered to a castle amused her.

Could pizza be delivered to a castle?

"What have you written?"

Maylie blinked hard and glanced at Rana. "Oh, well, I–I've written a lot but never . . . really finished anything."

"Oh, I see," Rana said. "Writing isn't easy. That's for certain. But that's why we're here now, isn't it?"

Maylie nodded and smiled at Rana. She smiled back with kindness in her eyes like Sarah. Maybe Maylie had just made a new friend.

The door opened then, and a tall, slim mustached man entered the room. She turned her attention to the man, who arranged items out of a briefcase. From the closer view, Maylie noticed he was much younger than she thought–probably Aunt Layla's age.

The man stopped arranging and glanced up to survey his students.

"Good afternoon everyone. I am Dr. Marcus Pennington. You may call me Dr. M. I'm not a medical doctor, I assure you. The sight of blood makes me churlish," he said with wide eyes.

Maylie, Rana, and a few other kids laughed.

"I am, however, a Professor of Literature at Oxford University, the birthplace of quite a few literary geniuses. Perhaps you've heard of *The Chronicles of Narnia* and *The Lord of the Rings*. Their authors–C.S. Lewis and J.R.R. Tolkien–were both Oxford professors and good friends. The two, along with others, formed a group called The Inklings to discuss writing. Having friends who share your interests is important, especially with writing. It is quite a solitary task, and it is nice to have someone who understands this."

Maylie and Rana smiled at each other.

"Jolly good. Now, let's talk specifically about writing. Who can name the most valuable tool we have as writers? Anyone care to have a go at it?"

A boy raised his hand.

"All right, young man. What is it?"

"A pen!" he exclaimed, hoisting one above his head in triumph.

The whole class erupted into laughter. Maylie saw Dr. M fighting to keep back a smile. The boy's face flared red.

"Good show, lad. I do agree that a pen is quite necessary, but it is not the answer I seek."

The boy grinned.

Dr. M continued, "The answer, students, is

your imagination. It is truly a most powerful thing. And to write you must tap into it."

He cleared his throat. "There are many types of writing. For this class, we will discuss fiction. Who can tell me what it is?"

The room fell silent. After another moment's hesitation, Maylie's hand shot into the air.

"Yes?" Dr. M nodded his head toward her.

"Fiction is stories about people and events that are made up."

"That's correct." He gave a slight smile. "Fiction may have true elements to it such as real locations and people from history. But the storyline overall is made up in fiction."

Dr. M shuffled a few papers on the table. "Fiction works with the writer usually prompted by something that has happened. Then, your imagination expands it to new possibilities. You can, of course, have an idea solely out of your own thoughts. But even so, the spark for the story in some way comes out of a writer's surroundings."

Maylie sat up straighter. The spark of a story. *That was it!*

The inspiration she had to find in Europe.

He paused and swept his hand toward the room. "There are story ideas all around you. Be observant, and you'll find that great idea."

Maylie glanced around the room and met the eyes of her brother. He looked away.

I could write about an annoying brother. She rolled her eyes and faced Dr. M.

"Now, once an idea sparks you must decide the story's genre. Whether it is historical fiction or mystery, science fiction or fantasy, humor or horror."

Maylie noticed the boys at the next table perk up.

"Yes, I thought horror might spark your interest. Let's try a few writing prompts. Please take out a sheet of paper and a pen or pencil."

The fluttering of paper on desks filled the air. "Each person will have one prompt to write." He moved through the room and handed out slips of paper.

Maylie clasped hers with both hands–*describe your first impression of a time-traveling postman who steals food from a dinosaur.*

Maylie leaned over to Rana. "My prompt doesn't make sense. What did you get?"

Rana let out a squeak when Maylie showed her the prompt. "Mine isn't any better." She held it out–*write a diary entry about a sneaky mermaid who wants to own a fish restaurant.*

A mermaid and a fish restaurant?

"Yours is worse than mine," Maylie exclaimed. "These are ridiculous."

Rana glanced above Maylie's head and gasped. Maylie turned to see Dr. M standing there. She sucked in a breath.

"Quite so," he said with a grin. "The exercises are a bit far-fetched, but they're meant to stretch the imagination."

Maylie's face cooled, and she smiled. "Mission accomplished."

Dr. M patted her shoulder. "Get to work now, girls."

Rana immediately scribbled on her paper while Maylie felt the familiar freeze of her mind as she urged her imagination to take her far away.

But twenty minutes later, she longed for a black hole to appear underneath the table and devour her.

Chapter Nine

Where to Next?

I only wanted to own a fish restaurant, and I had to serve what I had, which happened to be my cousins–the clownfish."

Dr. M clapped as Rana finished reading her story. "Well done, Rana. Very clever."

The other students clapped, and so did Maylie, but it was as if she were a robot programmed to imitate others. Her hands moved without thinking.

Dread filled her, and she slid her notebook over the top of her piece of paper that was still just as empty as it had been before.

She hadn't written a single word! And now it was *her* turn!

"Next," Dr. M said and moved his focus off Rana to her.

Maylie ducked her head and gripped the desk's edge. She couldn't meet his eyes or anyone's eyes. Her palms began to sweat, and her breaths sped up. She could feel her pounding heart and hear its rhythm in her ears as a rush of dizziness shot through her head.

"Umm . . . I–" She heard her voice as if she were faraway. She would try to explain, but the words wouldn't come. They were stuck so very deep in her throat she couldn't push them out.

"No worries. Why don't we skip you for now." She heard Dr. M say as if he were faraway too.

Maylie dared to look up at him. He smiled at her and moved on to the next student, who began to read their story and to Maylie's relief his words sounded less faraway than they had before.

She could feel Rana looking at her, but she couldn't look back.

How was she ever going to become a famous author?

It was hopeless. She couldn't do it, would never do it. Even Camden, her not-caring-about-the-class brother had written something.

She had tried so hard and thought and thought of the perfect start to the story, but nothing had been good enough in her head. She even had tried to think of how her favorite authors would have written it, but before she had known it, time was up, and the bright white empty paper stared back at her.

And Rana's story was perfect. She remembered how quickly Rana had started writing. It, no doubt, came easy for her. But *not* for Maylie.

Heat flooded her neck and face until she felt like fireworks were shooting out of her ears. She stared at her notebook so hard that the unicorn came to life before her eyes. Then, it morphed into a cat. She watched it curl up into a little silver ball just like Sparkles had days before.

Tears welled in her eyes. She squeezed them shut. If only she could wish herself back home to her safe and familiar room. She imagined that hole under the table as a portal to home. That she could fall through it and land on her soft bed beside Sparkles and out of the horrible room.

She opened her eyes again to stare at the cat, but before it could come to life again movement caught her attention. A slim tan hand slid something in front of her on the table. When it retreated, Maylie saw a colorful sticker of an adorable cat with rainbow fur.

Despite how she felt, she smiled and realized how far she had fallen into the *extreme zone* again. Deeper than usual.

Maylie wanted to flee, but for the rest of the class she sat frozen unable to even look up. She stared at that sticker.

As class ended, she slowly released her grip on the table. Dr. M hadn't called on her again. She blew out a breath.

"Students, smashing job! You have exactly what it takes to write–imagination. Remember though, sometimes it can run away with you. Use it wisely. This concludes our class. Happy writing to you all."

Maylie gathered her things. When she picked up the sticker, she hesitantly faced Rana. Dr. M's praise for Rana's writing still echoed in her mind.

She half-heartedly mumbled, "Thank you."

"Nice to meet you, Maylie," Rana said with a warm smile and finished gathering up her things. "Best of luck with your writing!" She waved at the doorway before she left the room.

Maylie heard her name called. It was Dr. M. "Don't forget this." He held out a writing packet.

His expression was knowing when he met her eyes. "And don't worry about the prompt. It was simply a silly exercise." He pointed to the packet. "But really dig into this. It'll help. And don't give up. Keep writing even if it's difficult. Really search out the possibilities."

Maylie wanted to ask what that meant exactly, but instead she only thanked him. She hugged the packet to her chest. "I'll try." But her voice was limper than a wet noodle.

If she didn't believe in her writing, who did?

She honestly didn't know how a packet would help–or offer these possibilities he'd talked about. She kept failing at writing.

She *was* a failure.

Dr. M gave a brief nod. "Good luck! And please tell your aunt I said hello."

Maylie's lips parted. *He knows Aunt Layla?*

She mumbled, "Okay," and he walked away as Grandma Suey approached her. She put an arm around Maylie's shoulders and glanced at Camden. "Did you have a good time?"

"No way." Camden shoved his hands into his pockets and passed them to leave.

Maylie ignored her brother. "It was fine."

"Just fine?" asked Grandma Suey with eyebrows lifted high.

Maylie didn't care to discuss it, and Grandma Suey must have taken the hint because she didn't say anything else.

On the Tube, Maylie stared straight ahead. This time it wasn't because of what Sarah called the *extreme zone* but more like the *mean zone*. And Rana was the main subject of the not-so-nice thoughts like turning Rana into an ostrich or Rana being sucked into outer space.

Maylie squeezed her eyes shut.

No, she didn't want anything to happen to Rana, but she did want to do all she could to beat her at writing.

Maylie had to be a better writer than her. She had to keep going and keep writing no matter what. But she would be the best even if it hurt.

Maylie scooted the armchair closer to the hotel window. She plopped into the cushy chair and propped her notebook on her knees. She uncapped the pen and tapped it on the paper.

Thwack. Thwack. Thwack.

She stared out of the window into London's city lights. *Come on ideas.* She squinted until the twinkling lights blurred.

Nothing happened. She closed her eyes and went back through the day's activities. Nothing stood out as a writing idea.

So instead of writing, her blank page filled

with scribbles of her name all over the page.

My amazing idea will come, she told herself, *and I'll be glad I practiced my signature for all the books I'll sign one day.*

Maylie nodded in satisfaction and put the notebook away at the exact moment her aunt burst into the room.

"Hi, everyone! Sorry I'm late." Aunt Layla kicked off her shoes and slung her purse onto the dresser.

Maylie hopped onto the bed with a bounce. Her aunt sank down beside her. She laid back and closed her eyes. "It's been a busy day for both of us." She sat up and looked at Maylie. "How was your class?"

"It was good," Maylie said though she couldn't tell the truth. "Dr. M said hi."

"Oh, Marcus, yes! I haven't seen him in months. He's a great guy."

"He's really nice," Maylie said and took note of the gleam in her aunt's eyes. *Hmm . . .* "What did you do today?"

"Meetings, more meetings, and making our travel arrangements." Aunt Layla sat up and so did Maylie.

This was the news she needed today–a new adventure. "Where are we going?" Maylie bounced up and down. "When?"

"I have a photo assignment, so we'll spend the next few days at–" Maylie eagerly looked at her aunt. "–one of the most amazing castles in England."

Maylie squealed and hugged Aunt Layla until they both fell back onto the bed.

I'm going to a castle—an actual real-life castle!

Chapter Ten
No Time for Games

Is it real? Maylie blinked. It was still there. She snapped a photo.

High walls stood strong of golden stone with more lining the top edges like jagged teeth jutting into the sky. Slim towers rounded each corner. The castle was like something from a storybook perched on an island with water spreading out in a wide moat.

Maylie could imagine archers at the ready to defend the castle with bows drawn and arrow tips sticking out between the roof stones.

She searched for knights in armor on horseback. She could almost see one at the structure's only entrance across a bridge rising above the small lake.

Brave knights once stood at that exact spot to fight and protect the beautiful lady hidden behind its walls.

"That is so cool," Camden exclaimed from beside Maylie. "I hope there's a torture chamber in the dungeon."

Maylie scoffed. "Where would it be? Underwater?" She turned her back on him and studied the castle.

"I don't *know*," he said with a sharp edge to his voice. "There should at least be ghosts or something in there. And I'll make sure they get you."

Maylie huffed and stomped away from him.

Doesn't he think about anything else except dumb scary stuff?

"It's known as the loveliest castle in the world." Aunt Layla handed Maylie a brochure. "It's certainly one of my favorites."

Maylie opened the tri-fold paper to vibrant images of the castle, a beautiful flower garden, a white owl, and the bright green hedges of an elaborate maze.

Something clinched in her chest. She jerked her head up. "There's a *maze*?"

Aunt Layla grinned. "Yes, and an exceptional one at that. Very unique."

Maylie surveyed her surroundings. "I don't see it anywhere."

Her aunt pointed past the castle. "It's far over that way. The castle is surrounded by over 500 acres of land. That's about 400 football fields."

"Whoa." Camden appeared around Aunt Layla. "We'll never see all that in a few days."

Aunt Layla placed a hand on his shoulder. "No worries, Cam. We'll hit the highlights."

Maylie smiled. Three days ahead of her at a fairytale castle and a maze. She couldn't wait. Her best friend, Sarah, would be so jealous. Maylie would be sure to take a lot of pictures.

"What do we do first, Aunt Layla?" Maylie asked and handed back the brochure.

"We tour the castle."

"Whoop!" Camden yelled. He jogged past Maylie and tagged her shoulder. "Last one there gets left in the dungeon!" He grinned and raced ahead.

Thrilled by the challenge, Maylie took off after him but then stopped in her tracks. She looked at her aunt studying the brochure. On second thought, she was *too* old for Camden's games.

Far ahead, she watched him reach the entrance. Hands on his knees, he drew a deep breath and glanced over his shoulder at her.

Even at the distance, Maylie saw his eyes narrow and darken with what looked like pain. But, of course, she was wrong because the next second his mouth twisted into a scowl, and he stalked forward with crossed arms.

He'll never grow up, Maylie thought. *Like Peter Pan.*

Camden had accused Maylie for months of never doing anything fun. But the real problem was their *idea* of fun had changed. That was it, she told herself again, because she had changed. She wasn't a little kid anymore.

Maylie, Grandma Suey, and Aunt Layla followed Camden to the gatehouse. Its giant studded wooden doors lay ajar.

Passing through them, Maylie stopped to snap a photo of a huge metal lion head on the door's center. Aunt Layla called out that it was a doorknocker, which explained the large ring in its mouth. It looked fancy and a bit scary at the same time, perhaps warning away all those who wished to enter.

She shivered and not from the cool breeze pushing across the water. She pulled her jacket tighter around her and jogged to catch up with the others.

A large oval lawn lay ahead in front of the castle's grand front entrance. The grass was very short with defined lines where the mower moved back and forth and reminded Maylie of a light green checkerboard. The group walked the curve of the pavement around the roped off grass.

The castle loomed in front of Maylie. She couldn't take her eyes off it as they traveled *up, up, up* to the tower tops. She imagined a princess locked up there.

Smack! Her thoughts skidded to a stop when she crashed into her brother's back.

"Ouch!"

"Oww!" he said and whirled to face her. His angry eyes and scowl were back. "Watch where you're going."

"Sorry, it was an accident."

He let out a grunt. "I bet." He lifted his chin and turned back around.

Maylie clinched her fingers into fists at her sides. She gritted her teeth.

Ooh, he makes me so mad.

Aunt Layla caught her eye and frowned.

Maylie shrugged and let out a huff of breath. She would not let her brother ruin her first ever visit to a castle. Not a chance.

She focused her attention on the smiling woman waiting for them in the tall arched doorway. "Good morning. I'm your tour guide, April," the woman said while keeping the smile. Maylie wondered how she talked and smiled at the same time.

"We would like to welcome you to Leeds

Castle–where there's discovery at every turn." She winked at Maylie and pressed on. "Leeds Castle is over 900 years old."

Maylie tuned out the rest for the moment. She looked up again.

Nearly 1,000 years old? Impossible . . .

Maylie didn't realize her mouth was hanging open until April looked at her and asked, "Are you okay, love?"

"Y–yes. I just can't believe this place is that old. How does it stay together?"

April grinned. "Very carefully. With a lot of cellotape."

Maylie laughed.

"But the truth is stone structures are quite strong. They, of course, had to withstand attacks. Parts of the castle are not of the same age. In 1660, half of it fell into the moat."

"Whoa," Camden said with awe on his face.

"Not if you were inside it, Cam," Maylie threw back with a glare.

"Yes," said the tour guide. "You would have had quite a shock if you'd been on the loo."

Maylie, April, Aunt Layla, and Grandma Suey chuckled. Camden stared at them until Aunt Layla informed him a *loo* was a bathroom.

"*Oh,*" he said and started laughing.

April clasped her hands. "Shall we continue the tour?"

Maylie nodded and eagerly followed her inside the castle.

Chapter Eleven

A Mysterious Sighting

Room after room, April guided them and offered information about each one and the castle itself.

Camden kept asking about knight's armor and medieval weapons until Maylie elbowed him in the ribs and whispered, "This isn't the Tower of London, Cam."

Maylie admired the intricate floral wallpaper in several bedrooms and how it even covered a room door concealed in the wall. She also liked the tiny but tall square courtyard with a small fountain at its center.

The staircase was another favorite feature–dark wood with a twisting handrail in the center that resembled a unicorn's horn pointing straight up.

Maylie stopped in the next room and glanced out the window. She took in the view and spied people below her on the grass. A boy and girl about her age stood outside near a woman on a cell phone. The girl wore a bright pink jacket. She had a camera aimed at a peacock, but the boy jumped in front of her, and the peacock flew away.

Maylie saw the girl furiously wave her hands at the boy, and then rush to the woman, who held up a hand to her.

The girl put up the camera and took out a notebook. Maylie's hands froze on the windowsill, and she leaned closer until she almost touched the glass with her nose.

No way... She was certain she knew that notebook and the dark-haired girl who held it.

Could it really be Rana?

Maylie heard her name and looked behind her to see Aunt Layla. "I'm coming." But when she glanced back out the window, there was no one there.

Was her imagination playing tricks on her?

Maylie caught up with the group just as Camden asked the tour guide, "Is there a torture chamber? Or any ghosts?"

April smiled at him. "Sorry to disappoint, but no. However, several people were imprisoned here including Queen Joan of Navarre. And a duchess was on trial here for witchcraft. But, besides the maze grotto, there's nothing particularly spooky here."

Camden appeared disappointed up until the point she mentioned the grotto. "What's wrong with the maze *grot-toe*?" He annunciated and looked at Aunt Layla. "And what is it?"

April explained that the *grotto* was like a cave at the maze's center that led to the exit. She added, "It is home to the Guardian of the Grotto and other eerie creatures who guard the maze."

Maylie shivered but pushed the images out of her head when they walked into a library of floor to ceiling bookshelves filled with dozens of old books.

The room held a crisp clean scent with a hint of leather. Velvety chairs were tucked around the room and looked so comfortable that Maylie longed to sink into one with a book.

"Let's go." Camden muttered and herded her out of the room. "I'm hungry."

Maylie narrowed her eyes. "You're always hungry." She took a final glance behind her at the room and followed the group to the exit. The tour concluded, and they thanked April.

Then, Aunt Layla led them away from the castle. She pointed to the pond on her right, and an odd black boat with swans on the side gliding through the water. "That's the Black Swan Ferry."

Maylie stared at it a moment and quickly looked away. She preferred to keep her feet on land.

Camden shrugged and marched on ahead past the sign that pointed toward the Castle View Restaurant. He called out, "After I eat, can we go to the maze and grotto thing?"

Aunt Layla said yes, and a shiver ran up Maylie's back when she thought about what April said. She *must* see this maze.

After a short walk, they took a seat outside the

restaurant at an umbrella-covered table and ate hamburgers and *chips*, well French fries.

Whoa, she thought, *do British people use a lot of strange names for things.*

Maylie finished her *chips* and went to throw her trash in the rubbish bin when she spotted the same girl from the window. She stood across the courtyard next to the museum entrance and a woman who spoke to an employee. The girl turned to the boy beside her. Maylie gasped.

It *was* Rana.

She couldn't believe it. Of all the places in the country and the world, the girl who had bested her at writing was right there in front of her.

The boy said something to Rana, and she looked away with a frown. Then, she met Maylie's gaze, and her eyes automatically widened.

Uh-oh, she'd been recognized.

Rana walked briskly toward her. "Wow, Maylie, I didn't think I'd see you again. And here you are!"

Maylie managed a smile as her brain fought

between fueling her jealousy or her genuine like for the friendly girl. "Me either. What are you doing here?"

"My mum works here." Rana looked at the woman still in conversation. "She oversees events and activities. I did say I lived near a castle in Kent." She laughed and spread her hands out. "And this *is* Kent. But what are *you* doing here?"

Maylie told Rana about her aunt's job, and then Aunt Layla came up to them. "How do you two know each other?"

Maylie explained about the writing class. Then, Rana's mother walked over and greeted Aunt Layla by name.

Introductions were made for Maylie, Camden, and Grandma Suey to meet Rana's mother, Vayu Peterson, and her older brother, Ravi.

"It's nice to meet you, Maylie. Rana has told me much about you." She put an arm around Rana's shoulders. "You made quite the impression on her."

She'd made an impression?

Maylie's smile was sheepish at best. Well, so had Rana, yet in Maylie's eyes it wasn't necessarily a good one. She blurted out the first thing that came to mind. "We both love cats."

Maylie wanted to crawl into a hole or ride away on the back of a giant cat or anything to get out of the situation.

"That you certainly have in common," said Rana's mother.

Then, Aunt Layla piped up. "Perhaps Rana and Ravi would like to go to the maze with us? We're heading there now."

Rana looked expectantly at Maylie. "I would love to. You'll simply adore the maze, Maylie. It's the best one I've ever seen."

Maylie avoided Rana's friendly gaze and merely nodded. How many mazes had Rana seen anyway? She had seen exactly *zero*.

Ravi chimed in that he wanted to go too, and Camden looked relieved to not be the only boy for a change.

Maylie wasn't getting out of this one. But at least it wasn't anything to do with writing, right?

Deep down, Maylie had to admit it wasn't

Rana that she didn't like but how easy writing–clever writing–came to her.

Rana huddled close by Maylie as they left the restaurant area and past a lovely flower garden. A yellow butterfly hovered by her shoulder. "How long is your stay?"

"Two more days. Until the concert."

"That's brill! Perhaps, we can spend time together. I'll ask Mum. There is quite a lot to do here. I would love to show you around, *and* we can talk all about writing."

Maylie swallowed hard–the one subject she was determined *not* to discuss with Rana. She was thinking of a reply when she stopped in her tracks and stared downhill at a huge sprawling tangle of dark green.

The maze.

People wove through tall hedge-lined pathways and others stood at the maze's center high up on a stone structure and called out to others below to guide them.

Rana laughed. "And it's as hard to complete as it appears." She raised her eyebrows. "But I'm up for the challenge if you are."

Maylie was about to reply when Camden and Ravi raced past them toward the maze and straight through the entrance.

Rana and Maylie exchanged glances. *Brothers.*

Grandma Suey said she would wait for them at the exit, and Aunt Layla went off with Rana's mom to talk business. The only thing left to do was go in.

Maylie propped her hands on her hips and studied the maze before her–hedges high overhead, and a path turning sharply in several directions.

Despite her uncertainty of spending time with Rana, her lips pulled into a grin, and the thrill of adventure coursed through her as she took her first steps into the maze.

Chapter Twelve
Beware the Grotto

Which *way to go?* Maylie looked left and right and straight ahead. She glanced at Rana, who shrugged, then took the left passage.

Maylie followed her and stuck out her right hand to drag it along the prickly green leaves. She'd read about that in a book once. Her shoes crunched on the path of white crushed stone as she picked up her pace into a light jog.

Surrounded by green with the blue sky above, she couldn't think of anywhere else she would rather be–definitely not Jasmine's water park– though she wished Sarah could be with her.

A breeze rustled the nearby hedge's leaves, and she heard Rana laugh and take off running, her feet sliding on the rocks. In a sudden burst of energy, Maylie rushed after her.

She dashed into the next passage, her hair whipping across her face. Dodging two teenagers, she rushed on and heard Rana's footsteps not far ahead of her. She also heard a woman's voice projected over speakers and knew it was the birds of prey area because she talked about an owl. Aunt Layla told her they would see the falconry show the next day. Her brother couldn't wait.

Where was he? In fact, she hadn't seen a glimpse of Camden or Ravi since they ran ahead into the maze. She shrugged and moved on.

After two more turns, she saw Rana skid to a halt in front of a solid wall of green leaves. A dead end. Maylie tried to stop, but her sneakers slid. She plowed right into Rana and sent them both sailing to the ground.

The urge to laugh welled up inside Maylie with such force that it burst from her chest like a firework. She rolled over to face Rana, who was laughing just as much. They sat up and brushed leaves and dirt off their clothes.

"Hold still, Maylie," Rana said with a giggle. She tugged something from Maylie's hair, held up two little twigs, and said, "You looked like a stag.

Complete with antlers," which brought more laughter.

In a moment, they were up and rushing forward through the maze, wheeling this way and that until they were horribly lost. But, to Maylie, it was one of the best afternoons of her life.

She wasn't sure how long it had taken them. But, after some help from people at the tower and Rana recognizing a part of the maze, they burst out of the hedged walkway to see the enormous stone tower looming above them.

Another burst of energy seized Maylie. She grabbed Rana's hand and ran up the curving staircase. Gasping for air, they reached the top and leaned against the rock wall to peer out over the maze they had just conquered.

The view stole Maylie's breath even more–

perched high like a bird in a tree able to see all around her, up and down, left and right over the maze. She looked for Camden and Ravi but didn't see them anywhere, though she did pay back the favor and call out directions to a few people.

She noticed a playground with a large wooden castle that looked like the actual castle. Kids ran across a rope bridge, and she thought of Jayna. She would've loved it. Thinking of her little sister reminded Maylie of her promise. She must go shopping soon!

Rana's voice broke through Maylie's thoughts. "Are you ready to face the *spooky* grotto?" She raised her eyebrows.

Maylie lifted her chin, and in a dramatic voice said, "I was born ready," which made Rana giggle as they descended the tower. Maylie smiled and followed her all the way around until she entered a tiny dimly lit cave-like room. She paused at the top of a spiral staircase that led *down, down, down* into the lair of the Guardian of the Grotto.

She glanced left and nearly jumped.

Two faces carved out of the rough wall glared at her with holes for eyes lit with pale blue light.

Two mermaid-like creatures of stone stared with faraway expressions on their scaly faces. Maylie shuddered.

It wasn't just the eeriness of the creatures, but the cool, wetness of the air and the sound of wind blowing up from the cave's depths followed by the noise of clanging metal.

The rough stone that enclosed them appeared to have a seashell and coral design, at least from what she could tell with the soft lighting of blues and pinks slanting across the walls.

Was this some sort of underwater Neverland?

The stairs ended in a large room. The sound of rushing water filled her ears. On the right, alcoves lit up in blue housed four more life-size female sea creatures with twisted spiky crowns and mouths open in an oval as if blowing furious gusts of winds into the room.

The figures, both beautiful and mysterious, mesmerized Maylie. She stepped up to the first one and reached out to touch it, then thought better of it. She turned left and leapt back in fright.

A gigantic stone face illuminated in sickly green light glared at her. Its eyes and mouth glowed red, and its gaping mouth gushed water into a pool below that sparkled with hundreds of coins.

The Guardian of the Grotto.

Maylie sucked in a hard gulp of air and stepped back.

"He looks friendly, right?" Rana called from behind her.

"Not at all."

Maylie's gaze moved up past the face to the low dome ceiling covered in rectangles of coral and shells forming  the outline of swans–the symbol of Leeds Castle. A much better sight to focus on.

"Maylie, this way," Rana said and pointed down another staircase. "The exit isn't far."

Maylie gave a final glance behind her. A chill still lingered. She shivered and walked down the staircase after Rana.

Something lurched from the shadows toward them. They screamed and stumbled backward. Maylie's heart leapt to her throat.

Then, her fear changed to face-on-fire anger as Camden and Ravi ran from them down a long tunnel. Hysterical laughter echoed off the walls.

In the darkness, Maylie heard Rana's rapid

breath and a low, guttural groan that sounded more like a growl.

Maylie clinched her fists. *My brother is going to get it!*

The rest of the grotto was lost on her. She stomped through it until she reached sunlight.

The only thing she noticed was a strange, stone creature, imprisoned by metal bars, with bulging eyes, a large flat nose, and what looked liked leaves growing from its face.

And, suddenly, she had a very good idea.

Chapter Thirteen
Writing a Secret

W ould you pass the sugar please?" Maylie asked Rana in her most polite grown-up voice.

Rana passed the little bowl of sugar cubes, but she gave Maylie a look. "Okay, *now*, will you tell me this brilliant idea?"

Maylie shook her head. "Not yet. Would you explain this?" She moved her hand over the table in front of them. "You're the one who invited me to afternoon tea, but I have no idea what to do besides make sure I have plenty of sugar."

Rana instructed Maylie on how to prepare the steaming hot tea in its delicate little cup of gold flowers and matching saucer. Then, she explained that the treats in front of them were scones to be filled with strawberry jam and clotted cream.

"Clotted cream?" Maylie's eyes widened. The jam looked like jelly and the scones like little breakfast biscuits, but the cream sounded weird.

"It's really good. Though, I do realize it may sound odd." She put a little of it on a spoon and held it out for Maylie to try.

Maylie took the spoon, studied the creamy spread, and licked a little off. *Hmm . . .* it reminded her of a cross between whipped cream and cream cheese, and it didn't taste bad at all.

With an expression of triumph, Rana showed Maylie how to split the scone in half and spread a layer of cream and jam in it. Then, they both held them daintily with their fingertips and took a bite.

Maylie wiped cream from her mouth. "I think

I could get used to this, even though the word 'clotted' is involved." Maylie grinned and followed Rana's example, carefully sipping her tea. The warmth and sweetness flooded her mouth. It was different but not bad.

She reached for another scone. Rana playfully slapped her hand away.

"Hey! What was that for?"

Rana folded her arms. "You promised to tell me the idea."

"Right." Maylie straightened in her chair, and so did Rana, her golden eyes focused intently on Maylie. She wasn't ready for this part of her idea.

"Well, about our writing class." Maylie traced the rim of the teacup with her finger. "It's just that.

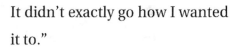

It didn't exactly go how I wanted it to."

Rana lightly touched her arm, and she looked up to meet her eyes. Her expression was like her friend Sarah's when she wanted Maylie to feel better about something. It spurred Maylie on in her explanation.

"It was embarrassing." Maylie hung her head. "And I'm sorry that I wasn't very friendly after class. I was jealous about how good your story was. I've tried so hard to write a story, and I just can't. But it's what I want most in the world."

This time, Rana took Maylie's hand and squeezed it. "It's okay. I understand. It's all right, Maylie. You can do it."

Relief flooded Maylie, and she smiled. "Maybe you could help me then. If that's okay?"

"It's more than okay." Rana's eyes brightened. "In fact, why don't we start a writing group."

"Fantastic idea! Like Dr. M said those two famous authors did. *Err* . . . what did they call it?"

"The Inklings," Rana said without hesitation, and then she gasped. "And I know what we can call ourselves–*The Pennies*. As in, we are girls, and we write with pens."

Maylie's face lit up. "That's perfect!"

"Thank you, thank you," Rana said with a little bow. "Now, is that *all* of your idea?"

"Not exactly. But combined with our writing group idea it completely fits because our first writing assignment–" She leaned closer to Rana and lowered her voice. "–should be about our brothers. To get back at them."

Rana turned up her nose with a *humph.* "That's right. And we shall meet in secret around the castle and grounds to write it." She drummed her fingers on the table. "But, what should it be about?"

Maylie beamed as she added the extra element of her idea. "It should be a horror story involving the maze and grotto. I think Camden and Ravi should be chased in the maze at night by monsters." She raised her eyebrows. "The monsters of the maze."

Rana's look of surprise quickly switched to one of glee. "Yes, let's do just that. When do we start?"

"How about right now?" Maylie took out her notebook. "Let's start thinking about it. What did Dr. M call that? Brain-thinking? No, brain-something . . ."

"*Brainstorming*," Rana declared triumphantly.

"That's right. We'll brainstorm over tea and then get to work. Why don't we go hide out in the playground after this?"

Rana nodded eagerly. Maylie could practically see the ideas whirling in her mind for their story of revenge.

After tea, Maylie and Rana perched with notebooks in hand on the swing near the replica wooden castle at the Knights' Realm Playground. Rana smiled. "How should we begin?"

Maylie tapped a pen on her notebook. "Maybe we should each start writing the beginning and see what direction we like the best."

"Good idea!" Rana said and like at the writing

class, she immediately started scribbling.

Once again, Maylie stared at a blank page. She tilted her notebook up, so Rana couldn't see. She swallowed hard and closed her eyes.

You can do this, Maylie. You can do this. Think.

How would her favorite authors write this story? What words would they use? Minutes later, she still hadn't written anything.

"What's wrong, Maylie?"

Maylie reluctantly met Rana's eyes and frowned. "I can't write. I've never even finished a story. I can barely start them."

Rana gently touched her arm. "I couldn't write either, Maylie."

Maylie's eyes grew wide. "Really?"

Rana nodded.

"But how can you write now?"

Rana offered a small smile. "I found my voice."

Maylie tilted her head. "Your voice?"

"Yes, my mum told me I had to write like me. In *my* words. Not someone else's. I'd tried to write like my favorite authors, but it never worked."

Maylie gasped. It was as if Rana had read her mind! "That's exactly what I've been doing. I thought if I wrote like them I *could* write a story."

Rana nodded. "Exactly. But it doesn't work because you're *not* them. You're Maylie. You have to write like Maylie."

She rummaged through her bag until she removed Dr. M's packet from the writing class. "There's a page about voice in the packet. Did you miss it?"

Maylie thought back to when she looked through it. She didn't remember that page. "Yes, I must have."

Rana showed it to Maylie. "It says to learn to find your unique author voice one exercise is to write a letter to your best friend about your favorite toy when you were five." She looked at Maylie. "You should do that. Right now."

128

Maylie tensed. "I don't know, Rana. I might not be able to do it."

Rana gave her a pointed look. "You can do it. Just think of how you talk to your best friend and write it down. Don't think too much. Just do it."

Maylie settled in her seat and pulled her notebook close. She sighed. "Okay, here it goes."

She stared at the blank page and froze. It couldn't be that easy. Write like herself?

But what if she wasn't a good writer? What if her words weren't good enough? She peered at Rana, who read a book. Rana believed she could do it. She had to try.

Don't think about it, Maylie. Just write a letter to Sarah.

And that's exactly what she did. She wrote Dear Sarah and set her mind on her best friend's face and wrote until the whole page was covered in words.

She looked up. "Done!"

Rana closed her book with a thud. "Great! Read it aloud please."

Maylie swallowed, but she read it.

When she was finished, Rana grinned. "That's it, Maylie. That's *your* voice. No one else can write just like you. You only have to remember that when you're writing a story. Just write the words in your mind that are already in there."

Maylie hugged Rana. "Thank you!"

Rana beamed at her. "I knew you could do it."

Maylie raised her eyebrows. "Now, let's get to work on *our* story."

The next morning was bright and sunny, and Maylie was in a very good mood. She waved to Rana and joined her on the bench by the Black Swan Ferry's dock. She watched it set sail for the first ride of the day.

"We missed the ferry." Rana pointed to the black boat lumbering across The Great Water as it was called. To Maylie the name fit even though it was probably not bigger than a large pond.

"Sorry," Maylie said with a shrug, though she was glad to miss it.

After her breakthrough at the playground the day before, she and Rana had written a whole page of story notes. This morning, they'd agreed to meet at the ferry and go back to the maze for what Maylie called "hands-on research."

"So, what do you think about this idea?" Rana

showed Maylie a page out of her notebook. "I thought it would be a nice twist." The gleam of mischief in her eyes was evident.

Maylie looked over the page and nodded. "I love it. I'll write it down later." She patted her bag. "We can go through the maze and grotto again, then work at one of the picnic tables. Let this meeting of *The Pennies* begin!" She gave Rana a high five.

Maylie watched a swan swim past the dock. Sun glistened off the water around it. She rested a hand on her bag, and excitement rose within her. The day sparked with magic.

Rana stood. "It's a lovely day but still a tad warm for my taste. We should buy ice lollies." Before Maylie could even show her confusion, Rana held up a hand. "I think you call them something like a pop icicle."

Maylie gave a little laugh. "A popsicle. And, yes, I'd love one." She stood up and followed Rana to the walkway. "Smashing idea!"

Rana grinned. "You're speaking like a Brit now."

"I'm trying." Maylie blew out a breath. "I never knew the same language could be so different."

Rana raised her eyebrows. "It is quite strange. Mum says it's like that with every language. Different countries, or even parts of a country, use different words." She flicked her dark hair over a shoulder. "And my mum would know. She speaks four languages."

"*Four.*" Maylie's mouth dropped. She couldn't imagine that many words swimming around in her head. As far as she knew, her dad only spoke two languages. Her mom knew only one.

"Yes. She was born in India, though she only lived there a few months, and then my grandparents brought her to live here in England. They taught her two languages from India–Hindi and Bengali. She also studied French at university."

"Does your dad speak more than one language too?" Though, Maylie was sure of one thing–she needed to learn more languages. She could converse some with her dad in Spanish, but she hadn't practiced in a long time.

Rana shook her head. "His side of our family has been in Britain a very long time. However, he did study German at university."

"Oh, so your dad's parents aren't from India?"

"No, he and Mum met at university. There are quite a lot of people like me here who are of Indian descent and part Indian too. India was owned by the United Kingdom for many years, so a lot of people from there came to live here. My dad told me his family has been in this country for hundreds of years."

"*Wow.*" Maylie stared at the garden full of flowers to her left. "I have no idea where my mom's family comes from–besides America, of course. But my dad is from Costa Rica. He speaks Spanish. It's kind of like with your mom. He was born there but moved when he was a little kid."

"Whoa, it seems we have something else in common. I know a little Hindi from my grandparents. Do you speak Spanish?"

"A little. Have you been to India? I went to Costa Rica when Cam and I were babies, but I, obviously, don't remember that. Dad says we might go for Christmas this year. That would be interesting."

"Yes, it would. We go to India once a year to see my aunts and uncles and all my cousins. I rode an elephant in the jungle last year."

Maylie's eyes widened. "A real-life elephant? No way!"

"Yeah, want to see?"

Maylie nodded, and Rana stopped at a picnic table to take out her tablet. She showed Maylie some photos and a video from India.

The bright colors that people wore, and the animals were amazing! Maylie wanted to go to India and ride an elephant too.

"I love India, but I agree with Mum. Everyone comes from somewhere, but where we decide to call home is the most important place."

Maylie smiled. "Your mum sure knows a lot."

Rana nodded, and then pointed ahead of them at the maze entrance. "There lies the lair of the monsters."

Without pause, they entered the gate, and Maylie allowed her mind to dive into her fictional world. What had Dr. M said? Search for the possibilities. Let her imagination go. She breathed in deep and focused.

Possibilities . . . what could she see happening next in the story?

What if a monster jumped out from this hedge? Or someone called out for help in front of her?

What if . . . and then it seemed the possibilities began to pour out in front of her. She quickly scribbled in her notebook.

Even in broad daylight, it was like she looked

down on the story playing out from above. She was there with Camden and Ravi as they made their way through the maze to the tower and then the grotto.

In the grotto, the Great Face still sent a chill through her along with the other creatures, and apparently, Rana too was affected because she quickly fled to the tunnel with Maylie not far behind.

And upon exiting the grotto Maylie knew exactly how the story would continue. The scenes whirled through her mind like a movie on a big screen. Her fingers itched to get it all down on paper. She obeyed them by plopping down at the closest picnic table and scribbling away while Rana bought ice lollies.

She wrote, and she wrote. She closed her eyes a moment, and then wrote some more. In fact, she was so engrossed in her notebook, she didn't see Camden and Ravi until they stood beside her.

"What's that?" Camden pointed at her story

and bent to read it.

Maylie jumped and closed the notebook with a *snap.* "Nothing," she said and slipped it into her bag.

He glared down at her. "Did that have my name on it?"

They can't know about this. I need a distraction. "Umm . . . it's something inspired by the trip. You know, writing stuff." She tried to keep her voice normal, but it was slightly high-pitched.

Camden narrowed his eyes. "Really?" he asked in a more interested tone than she liked.

What to do?

"So, what are you doing here?"

"Aunt Layla sent us to find you. It's time for lunch."

"Okay. I'll be there in a few minutes."

Rana walked up with the popsicles. Ravi spoke up then. "Come on. We're to meet Mum for lunch." He raised an eyebrow. "She won't think a lolly fits the bill."

Rana made a face at him and unwrapped one. She handed it to Maylie.

"Whatever," Ravi said with a shake of his head. "Let's go." He and Camden walked away.

Rana whispered to Maylie, "That was close."

Maylie nodded and blew out a huff of breath. Their brothers could *never* find out about the story.

Chapter Fourteen
Flight of Maylie

Spreading slim white and golden wings the snowy owl swooped from the sky and onto the man's gloved hand.

"This is Edie, a female wood owl. Wood owls are native to the U.K.," he explained to the crowd as she took off to land nearby on a tall tree stump. "She is only one of over two dozen different birds of prey we have here."

After lunch, Maylie met back up with Rana for a round of mini golf before joining their brothers and Grandma Suey at the Birds of Prey afternoon show. The owl opened its beak like it was yawning and shook its feathered head.

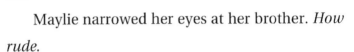

Maylie heard Camden whisper to Ravi, "I know how she feels. Where's the falcon?"

Maylie narrowed her eyes at her brother. *How rude.*

He ignored her and kept whispering about how boring the owls were until Grandma Suey nudged him with her elbow and said, "You keep this up, Cam, and you won't have your surprise today."

He jerked his head up. "Surprise?"

She gave him a look, and he turned back and appeared more interested in the show after that.

Maylie and Rana exchanged a glance.

Brothers.

She liked the owl with its curious heart-shaped face and dark eyes and small beak and that it was nocturnal. She liked to stay up late at night too, and she knew another nocturnal animal–her cat–who seemed to curl out of the little silver ball as soon as Maylie was going to sleep. Maylie had to hide the jingle ball, or the tinkling sound would keep her awake.

She thought about the stuffed cat that she slept with each night in place of Sparkles, and a twinge of homesickness fluttered her insides.

She and Camden video chatted with Mom, Dad, and Jayna every night before bedtime, so she'd seen them and Sparkles too, but it wasn't the same. Had she only said goodbye to them a week ago?

No, Maylie, you're okay. You are brave and adventurous and having a great time. You will not miss home.

She looked at Rana and thought of the story, and she watched as an owl flew right over the top of a volunteer's head. She glanced over at the maze. She was ten years old and in England at a castle on her first trip across "the Pond." Everything was going to be fine.

The birds performed for treats, flying up and down, from stump to stump, even landing near her on a wooden perch. The falcon's serious expression flicked left and right, and then it went back to the man.

Maylie hadn't seen anything like it before, and after the show she fought a bit of jealousy when Grandma Suey announced that Camden would spend the rest of the day with the falconer. But Maylie and Rana had other plans for the afternoon. Better plans.

They walked to the castle and hopped onto Elsie the Castle Train, a little bright green motorized train that zoomed over the walkway to the main entrance.

Maylie thought it was the cutest thing. She waved to people as they passed. They waved back.

She wrote more of the story. Rana offered up ideas at her shoulder.

At the gift shop, they got off, and Rana gave Maylie's bag to a smiling lady named Nancy for safekeeping while Maylie and Rana explored another part of the castle grounds–the Go Ape Tree Top Adventure.

Maylie nearly skipped alongside Rana as she talked about the ziplines and how high they would be in the air, and the thrill of it all sent a pulse of excitement and anticipation through her.

She spotted Aunt Layla up ahead with a strap contraption around her waist and legs. She talked to a man in a black shirt with a big orange logo on the back. Her aunt smiled and waved them over. "This is my niece, Maylie, and it's her first time on a zipline."

"Really now?" He looked at her and then at her feet. "I see you've got your trainers. Good girl."

Huh?

Rana whispered, "Your sneakers. We call them

trainers."

How do we speak the same language?

After being fitted for their harnesses and listening to a short class about rules and safety, Maylie pulled on her gloves. It was time.

She tried not to think about everything that could go wrong, but it didn't work. What if her harness broke and she fell from so high up? What if a huge purple bird landed on the line in front of her and she crashed into it?

Maylie shook her head. No, stop the *extreme zone.*

She followed Rana up a rope ladder to the practice course that wasn't very high off the ground. She focused on walking a tightrope like a circus performer.

Then, she climbed a much taller ladder to the actual course where they crawled through a big wooden barrel and crossed over a long rope bridge with spaced out wooden boards like something Maylie imagined would have been at the Lost Boys' camp in Neverland.

That was it. Pretend this *was* the Lost Boys' camp, and she was safe within the pages of a story.

Maylie didn't look down at first as they climbed higher, but she finally did when she held tight to the cables on each side of the bridge.

After the bridge, there was a series of obstacles with metal rings on the ends of ropes to step on, hanging logs to walk across, and many others. Maylie rested after the rings. She looked at Rana.

"Whew, my arm muscles are burning. I'm definitely not Tarzan."

"Up ahead there's a giant net we have to swing into, so you'll have to prove your Tarzan skills then."

A huge net?

And there it was–like a massive thick spider's web. Maylie shuddered. She stopped herself from looking around for a giant spider hiding in the trees and instead watched several kids and a few adults slam into the net and try to catch hold of it without success.

"You look nervous," Rana said in a low voice. "Just try to grab it. But it's okay if you don't."

"I know." Maylie looked at her friend. "What if I get all tangled up and hang upside down like a monkey? Will you rescue me?"

Rana gave a little laugh. "Sure, and we'll have a superb story to write about in our notebooks later. We'll call it 'Princess of the Apes'."

Maylie snickered.

Rana called out, "Toodle-oo!" and flung forward off the platform and into the net. She grabbed it on her second try.

Maylie looked over at her aunt, who gave an encouraging nod. "Here I go!" She closed her eyes and jumped. She readied her hands to grab the net. Her body hit the soft ropes and bounced back, but she grabbed hold of a strand with all her might–and it worked.

She opened her eyes, and Rana clapped. She did it!

Aunt Layla swung down with a Tarzan yell, and Maylie and Rana giggled. Then, they continued the course to their first long zipline. Rana volunteered to go first, and with harness and line secured by Aunt Layla, she rushed off the platform with a shout and flew–actually flew through the air–zipping like lightning to a distant tree.

Maylie's breath caught, and her aunt leaned down. "Don't worry. You'll be fine. You don't have to jump off like she did."

Maylie gave her a small smile. "Thanks, but I need to be brave and give it a try." Then, she sucked in a deep breath and jumped. Her feet lost the platform, and she looked down at them dangling high above the ground.

Her stomach dropped, and she looked forward. Her ponytail whipped against her neck, and a thrill rushed through her.

SHE WAS FLYING.

Her hands held tight to the harness strap as

she zoomed through the air to Rana. Her friend grew from a little speck in the distance.

What did the instructor say about landing?

She searched her mind, but nothing came. She had to do something! She put her feet out in time to catch herself on the ground. Her legs pushed forward in a sprint on the soft wood chips; though she realized the line caught her. She let out a held breath. "That was unbelievable!"

"I know," Rana said with a confident nod. "There are many more to come."

Maylie glanced ahead to more ziplines and tree platforms stretched a long way in front of them. She burst out in a wide grin. *This must be how Aunt Layla feels on all her adventures.* "All right. Let's go!"

When it was time for the next zipline and after clearance from Aunt Layla, Maylie was ready this time. Rana sailed away, and Maylie jumped with her arms out wide flying like Peter Pan and Wendy. She didn't want it to end.

"This one's the best," Rana said at the next platform. "Close your eyes and count to 10, then open them and get ready to be amazed."

Maylie squinted but couldn't see the other platform at all.

Maylie wasn't sure about closing her eyes, but she would try. She nodded as Rana took off and disappeared through the trees.

"Ready, Maylie?" her aunt asked after checking her gear twice.

She nodded, jumped, and closed her eyes as Rana instructed. This time her hands clasped tightly on the rope. Her body seemed weightless as she picked up speed and counted. At ten, she opened her eyes, and her mouth dropped. She sucked in wind and quickly closed it.

What a view.

The trees opened into a huge, bright green strip of land with no trees. It was like a big minus sign underneath her feet, and Maylie realized how high she was in the air. She probably could be looking out the window of a two-story building.

Her insides quivered. She scared away the butterflies and enjoyed the moment.

Maylie landed to Rana's cheering. She unhooked herself and ran over to give Rana a hug. Then, they both cheered as Aunt Layla zoomed in and gave them each a high five.

"You're quite the pro, Rana," she said and patted her shoulder. She wrapped Maylie into a big hug. "And, May, I knew you could do it."

Maylie beamed and hugged her right back very tight.

"Whoa, there. You're like an anaconda."

Maylie loosened her grip and started to laugh. "That's exactly what I told, Jayna, before we left."

Her aunt ruffled her hair. "Like aunt, like niece."

The instructor snapped a photo of them by a "Hurrah! You did it!" sign.

"I'm worn out." Maylie leaned against the sign. "I'm going to sleep like a baby tonight."

Rana nodded, and her stomach growled. "But, first, dinner. My stomach is worn out too."

They all burst out laughing. Maylie threw an arm over Rana's shoulders, and they followed Aunt Layla back to the gift shop.

Chapter Fifteen
Late Night Write

Maylie sat on the bed and patted her middle full of dinner. She lay back and sighed.

She'd eaten a whole plate of fish and chips . . . but not *chips. The words in this country.*

She shook her head. Her gaze focused on a tiny dent in the ceiling of their room at the Stable Courtyard Bed and Breakfast.

Grandma Suey had said it was like an inn in the old days when a building had a few rooms to rent to travelers. Maylie liked that it was in the middle of everything and not far from the maze. They also served a really good breakfast every morning in the restaurant.

Maylie shared a large bed with her aunt while Grandma Suey had the other one to herself. Camden slept on the sofa bed. He was there now wearing headphones and focused on his video game.

Grandma Suey sat on her bed and watched a TV show with men in checkered skirts. Maylie had no idea what that was about and wasn't sure she wanted to know.

She rolled over and grabbed her iPod and headphones from her bag. She listened to music while texting Sarah about ziplining. She left out about spending time with Rana though. She didn't want to make Sarah jealous or upset.

Sarah was her *best* friend. But Rana was starting to be another best friend. Maybe she could be her *best* writing friend.

Rana . . . She would miss her.

Tomorrow was their last day together before Maylie headed to a new country.

Maylie sat straight up. She must finish the story *tonight*. She'd surprise Rana with it.

She fluffed the pillows against the headboard and leaned back until she was comfortable. Camden was in full view, and if he came near her, she could quickly change to another page.

The low volume of the TV hummed in Maylie's ears until the sounds were unrecognizable. She read over the story notes and fell headfirst back into the story. Her pen moved with lightning speed.

She wrote and wrote while her aunt read a book beside her. She caught her aunt peeking over at her a few times.

"May, what has you so enamored?" She pointed to the notebook. "A story?"

Maylie nodded. "It's my first story since the writing class."

"Great!" Aunt Layla said with delight evident

on her face. "I can't wait to read it."

Maylie frowned a little. That wasn't a good idea. She might get in trouble.

Aunt Layla put a hand on her arm. "I'm sure your story is wonderful. Don't doubt yourself. You can do it."

That *wasn't* the problem, but Maylie didn't try to explain. Instead, she smiled and got back to work.

It seemed only minutes later it was time for lights out. She reluctantly put her notebook away and tried to settle down to sleep. She really did try.

Aunt Layla called her a "wiggle worm" from her tossing and turning. All the dialogue and story plot yet to be written floated around in her head. At that moment, Maylie wished she were much older than ten, so she could stay up late and write if she wanted.

She turned away from Aunt Layla and snuggled her face against the pillow. She shut her eyes and took a deep breath. She counted sheep.

She thought about boring things. Nothing worked.

Maylie listened to the breathing of the other three people in the room. She just *wasn't* tired. After a few more minutes of staring into the dark, she slipped out of bed, grabbed her bag, and headed for the bathroom. Maybe if she wrote a little more, she would be tired.

Yes, she'd only write a little bit and then be back in the bed before anyone would know. She sat with her back against the tub and wrote with her head bent low over the page, the words flowing faster than she could write them.

Maylie was back in the creepy, dark maze with her characters–running and running. One page filled up and then another and another as they tried to stay alive. She was near the end when a hideous creature sprang out of the darkness.

And it was in that moment, the bathroom door opened with a loud creak.

Maylie yelped and threw her notebook and pen into the air.

Grandma Suey appeared, and Maylie's head sank to her bent knees. She sighed in relief. Then, she realized she'd been caught.

"Maylie, it's nearly two o'clock in the morning. What are you doing up?"

Two a.m. She'd been writing over two hours. And she was near the end! The actual *end* of a story!

Maylie clenched her teeth unsure what to say. She retrieved her notebook where it was splayed open on the tile floor and looked up. "Sorry, Grandma Suey. I–I couldn't sleep and thought if I wrote I might be tired. I lost track of time."

"I see." Her grandma put a hand on her hip. "Well, you better run along to bed now."

"Grandma Suey?"

"Yes, Maylie."

She didn't want to ask it, but she felt she had to. "I'm almost done writing. Like really finishing a story for the first time ever! Could I have a few more minutes?" she pleaded. "Then, I promise I'll head right to bed."

Grandma Suey's face tightened and then relaxed. "Two minutes. And I mean it."

Maylie gave a sharp nod and scribbled into her notebook until she wrote THE END in huge letters at the bottom of the page.

She stared at those two words and couldn't believe her eyes.

Grandma Suey popped her head in through the door. "Two minutes are up."

Maylie scrambled to gather her things and got back in bed. She closed her eyes and took deep breaths.

She tossed and turned again and finally fell into a fitful sleep–but she wasn't alone.

The monsters of the maze were with her.

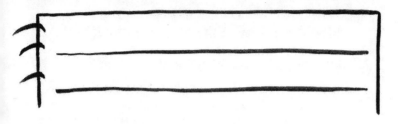

The Monsters
of the Maze

By Maylie Montes &
Rana Peterson

I'm not scared." Camden crossed his arms
and glared at his sister.

Maylie glared back. "Oh, yes, you are. I
bet you couldn't make it past the first turn
without peeing your pants."

Rana covered her mouth to hide her
laughter.

Ravi stood by Camden. "He wouldn't be afraid, and neither would I. In fact, I could go through the maze blindfolded."

"Oh, yeah?" Maylie put a hand on her hip and pointed to the entrance. "Then, go ahead. Prove us wrong."

Camden turned quickly and marched forward with Ravi at his side. "We'll show them."

Camden and Ravi easily climbed over the locked gate. Maylie and Rana walked up, and Maylie held out a flashlight through the bars.

"We don't want that," Camden said with a growl.

Maylie put it away. "Suit yourself. And good luck."

Ravi smirked. "We don't need luck."

The full moon was low overhead and flooded the path like a spotlight.

"Piece of cake," Camden muttered. He couldn't wait to see his sister's face when they not only made it out but also did it in record time. Her mouth would drop clear to the ground.

Ravi punched Camden in the shoulder. "Ready?"

"Yeah." Camden pumped his fist into the air. He turned to glare at his sister one more time.

What? His face fell. He blinked twice.

Only seconds ago, the gate had been there. But it was—it was gone.

His heart skipped a beat, and then it raced forward a little faster. He stared at what was now a dead-end of solid hedge. No gate in sight.

Camden shuddered. Had the air grown cooler? He shook it off. His mind was playing tricks on him. That was all.

His attention went back to the path before him where he knew they would take a left, and it would lead them out in no time.

But the moon slid behind a cloud, and as his eyes adjusted to the dim light, a chill shot through him, right through his blood. He didn't recognize the path at all.

Four narrow passages stretched before them and twisted off in all directions. From each one curled a thin, smoky fog that crawled low over the ground like skeletal fingers reaching out toward them.

Ravi sucked in a breath. Then, he cleared his throat quietly and whispered in a shaky voice, "No problem. We've only to find the tower at the middle. Then, we're out."

They both looked up to spot the tower, but it had disappeared behind thick fog.

Ravi grabbed Camden's arm. Camden jumped and almost yelled. Ravi pointed left. "Let's go that way."

Camden nodded. His eyes were too wide to be confident though. He inched forward with Ravi into the maze and down the left passage. The wind moved the hedge leaves like a soft, creepy breath.

Camden and Ravi huddled closer together in the middle of the narrow path. Their ears were alert to any sound other than the crunch of their own footsteps. Camden breathed out slowly to make as little noise as possible. But they heard nothing else.

They pushed on with left and right turns.

Ravi led the way, but Camden could tell he didn't know where he was going.

Somehow, this was a completely different maze.

After walking for what seemed like an hour to Camden, he grabbed Ravi's arm to stop him. "Did you hear something?"

Ravi narrowed his eyes to focus and shook his head. He started to walk again, but Camden froze. He'd heard something. He was sure of it.

Camden held his breath. And there it was—the extra crunch of footsteps after Ravi stepped. Camden rushed to catch up with him.

 Ravi stopped and leaned over to Camden. "I hear it now. Someone else is in the maze."

They paused and listened. Nothing but eerie silence until . . . footsteps not far away.

Camden stared at Ravi. Both their eyes were wide. Their breaths came fast. They took off running Camden right behind Ravi.

As soon as they turned the corner, they collided with something solid and fell to the ground with a groan.

They scrambled up. Their hearts raced. They were about to run when out of the shadows in front of them two large eyes popped open and out stepped a weird little man-like creature with a huge flat nose and leaves growing out of his face. He only stood about

as high as their stomachs.

Camden's mouth bobbed open and closed like a fish, but he couldn't get a word or a scream out.

The creature held up its hands. "Don't— don't be alarmed," he said in a fast, high-pitched voice. "Shh, shh . . . quiet." He raised a long slim finger to his lips. "Be quiet, or they'll hear you."

The fright in his eyes hit Camden and Ravi with instant fear.

"Who?" Camden whispered with trembling lips. "Who will hear us?"

The creature looked around and stepped closer. "The Stone Maidens who do his bidding."

Ravi crouched down. "Stone Maidens?"

"You don't understand." The creature wrung his hands and stared at them. "They sound like lovely creatures, but they certainly are not, certainly not." His head shook. The leaves swished.

"Who is he?" Camden barely got out.

"*He.*" The creature swallowed and gave a nervous glance left and right. "He is the Guardian of the Grotto. All who pass into his domain become his prey."

Camden grabbed Ravi's arm. "His prey?" A sick feeling settled in his stomach. "We gotta get out of here," he said in a panicky voice. He looked at the strange creature. "Do you know the way out?"

The creature's expression turned even more serious. "Yes. We must get the key. If we do, we are free." He held up a hand. "We must escape the maidens first."

"But how?" Ravi asked with a glance behind him.

"I can smell them." He took a great sniff of the air. His leaves shook, but he seemed satisfied. "They are not near."

"What are they?" Camden asked and looked around. He tried to calm his breathing.

"Oh, they are hideous, scaly creatures. They appear beautiful with long flowing hair and delicate faces, but they'll have you caught in their nets before you can blink. He sends them out to catch trespassers." He cleared his throat. "He has sent them for you."

"What about you?" Ravi narrowed his eyes. "Aren't you trespassing?"

"No, I escaped the grotto. They do not know." He straightened. "I am Valion the Tradari—but they call me The Green Man. I want to be free. We must help each other. We must get the key."

Camden looked at Ravi.

Ravi looked at him.

They didn't have another choice but to trust this strange creature.

"Let's get that key." Camden meant for the words to come out strong and brave, but his voice was weak.

Valion nodded. "Come with me. We go to the tower."

Camden and Ravi followed him and paused every few feet or so while Valion sniffed.

After a few turns, he froze. So, did Camden and Ravi. He pointed to the ground ahead. His voice was so low they could barely hear him. "It's a trap. We are close."

Camden squinted. He leaned closer and saw a string stretched across the ground. He watched Valion step over it, and they did the same. After another turn, Valion paused and sniffed. His thin body tightened. He stopped and stared ahead.

Camden's arm hair stood up. Goosebumps popped up on his skin.

At the end of the long passage ahead, he caught sight of a tall, slim creature from behind. Its high twisted crown like sharp teeth of a beast gleamed in the moonlight. A net was pulled behind it.

A Stone Maiden.

The creature slinked away from them and turned left.

Valion grabbed Camden and Ravi's arms and half pulled them forward and into the right passageway.

Camden gasped for air. His heart sounded like a fast drum.

Valion huddled them together. He spoke quickly. "We need a distraction. The tower is at the end of this passage." He pointed straight. "I'll run out of the passage first. After me, both of you run up the tower as fast as you can and grab the key. It's at the top in plain sight. You will see it."

Everything happened so fast Camden and Ravi could only nod.

Valion whispered, "Now!"

He took off running as fast as his short legs would go. Camden and Ravi waited a few moments and charged forward. Camden wasn't sure what they were doing except he knew he had to get that key.

Ahead, Valion yelled, "Come and get me!" Then, he gave a yelp. He may have sacrificed himself for them. They had to get that key and fast. The tower suddenly rose above them. They ran up the curving staircase taking two steps at a time with hearts pounding.

Nearly at the top, Ravi cried out. Camden turned to see a net thrown over his head, and he fell hard.

But Camden didn't stop. He pushed on. His legs and chest burned. He could see the top. He rounded the stairs and saw a giant metal black key floating over a big rock.

His breath caught.

His eyes met the ice-cold glare of a Stone Maiden. The shiver down his back pushed him forward with a leap through the air for the key. It jumped too with an ear-splitting screech.

He closed his eyes and held out his hand.

Metal touched his palm. He grabbed the

key and landed hard on the ground. He scrambled up and pumped it into the air. "We are free!"

The Stone Maiden stood tall and silent. Her attention was on the key. Then, Ravi appeared at the top. A spear was pointed at his back. He threw the net off and ran beside Camden.

Camden looked at him and then at the creature. "Where is Valion? What did you do to him?"

The Stone Maiden said nothing. She only pointed a grey scaly hand down the staircase.

Camden and Ravi shared a look and then walked down the stairs.

Another Stone Maiden stood at the bottom with her hand out toward a path on the left that led to a dark doorway. Camden and Ravi walked forward, and three Stone Maidens came behind them.

Camden kept a tight grip on the key. It was their ticket out.

They stepped through the doorway into a small room with dim lighting. He saw two faces carved into the wall with empty holes for eyes. He took a deep breath and went down the curved staircase.

It opened into a circular room with a high rounded ceiling decorated with carvings in the stone. The sound of rushing water was behind them.

Four empty spaces in the wall looked to be the exact size of the Stone Maidens. He also saw another doorway leading down to more stairs.

Was that the way out?

He glanced back to see if they were supposed to go on, but what he saw glued him to the spot.

A face. A gigantic stone face in the wall stared at him with glowing red eyes. A scream welled up in Camden's throat and stuck there. He couldn't make a sound.

It was he—the Guardian of the Grotto.

Water poured from its open mouth to a pool below. The mouth began to speak in a booming voice that shook the ground. "You have entered my maze. You have trespassed."

Ravi swallowed and spoke in a weak voice. "It—it was an accident. We—we didn't mean to trespass."

"Whether you did or did not is not the question. You are here. You must be punished."

Camden held up the key. "We have this. Now, you must let us and Valion, go free. We will never return."

The great face fell silent a moment, and Camden and Ravi exchanged a look. They had the key and were supposed to go free. Right?

A deep, rumbling sound shook the ground until laughter like thunder came from the giant mouth. The Stone Maidens joined in with high-pitched cackles. "You—you dare think I will let you go because of a worthless key? You are foolish."

Camden's mouth dropped. His knees grew weak, and his voice came out in a squeak. "But Valion said . . ."

"Not all should be trusted."

The familiar voice echoed through the room. Camden's head swam, and a sickening feeling came over him as Valion stepped from the shadows beside the great face.

His expression was cold and hard. He stared at Camden and Ravi, and then looked up at the face and bowed low.

"Oh, great Guardian of the Grotto, once again I have delivered those who dare trespass. Let them meet their fate but allow me to go free."

"You have done well, Valion, but your debt is not yet paid." The face looked at a Stone Maiden. "Lock him back up."

Valion muttered and stammered when he

was dragged away. The last thing they heard him say with a wicked gleam in his eyes was: "Be careful who you trust. Be careful who you trust."

The face looked at Camden and Ravi, and the mouth started to open wide. Their blood chilled. Panic rose inside them.

This couldn't be happening.

Camden's eyes searched the room for a way out. He went to rush for the door when he felt a huge shove from behind, and they both fell forward into the mouth and into darkness.

THE END

Chapter Sixteen
The Power of Imagination

*B*e careful . . . *Be careful who you trust . . . Be careful who you trust."* Maylie's whole body shook, and she set straight up in bed. Sweat coated her T-shirt, and tears slid down her cheeks.

She shook her head. She was in their room not the grotto. Everything was fine.

"Maylie, May . . . it's okay," Grandma Suey said in a soothing voice. Maylie let out a long, shaky breath and then realized that Grandma Suey held her shoulders. She buried her face into her

185

grandma's shoulder and cried like Jayna did with a scraped knee.

Grandma Suey patted her back and spoke softly to her. "It's okay. It's okay, sweetheart."

After a few minutes, Maylie calmed down and wiped her eyes. She was not in the maze or the grotto. There were no monsters after her.

Her dream was so real though–just like her story except she was in it.

Grandma Suey handed her a tissue. "You had a nightmare?"

Maylie nodded, but she didn't say a word.

A nightmare of her own creation.

Grandma Suey patted her shoulder. "Well,

you're okay now, right?" Maylie nodded again. "Aunt Layla and Cam already went down to breakfast."

Maylie breathed a sigh of relief. All she needed was Camden picking on her about crying. If he'd had a dream like that he'd be crying too. She washed her face and went to breakfast. Her mind was on the notebook in her bag. What would Rana think about it?

Then, the day's significance caught up to Maylie. It was their last day at the castle. It was her last day with Rana.

She remained quiet throughout breakfast, but she tried to cheer herself up and not think about the nightmare. She needed to enjoy the day and the night too—the big concert and fireworks display!

When Maylie, Camden, Aunt Layla, and Grandma Suey arrived at the castle, there were no tourists in sight. The park was closed to prepare for the concert. In fact, they were all helping set

187

up. But, first, Maylie would meet Rana at the castle.

Maylie spotted Rana's pink jacket when she entered the castle's gatehouse with the lion on the door. Rana turned and waved. They met on the walkway.

"Sorry, but we must help my mum fold and sort programs before we can finish the story," she said while they walked toward the castle entrance.

Maylie opened her mouth and then closed it.

"What is it?"

"I–I finished the story last night."

Rana's mouth dropped. "You did? That's brill!"

Maylie offered a half smile. "Yeah, I guess."

"You guess?" Rana raised an eyebrow. "What's wrong?"

Maylie swallowed her unease and smiled. "I, well, nothing," she said, hoping Rana would drop it.

Rana shrugged. "Okay, but I can't wait to read

188

it." She skipped ahead. "Last one to the door is a rotten egg."

Maylie rolled her eyes and took off after her.

When they rushed into the castle, Rana led her to the library, and Maylie's eyes grew wide. Rana's mom sat on the floor with what looked like a million papers around her.

Would they be done by tonight?

"All you do is stack the programs and place them neatly in the bins." She pointed to several large metal containers, then stood and handed Rana a stack of papers. "Time to get to work, love." She turned to Maylie. "Thank you for helping out."

"You're welcome." Maylie's attention was on the sea of paper.

Rana's mom noticed. "Don't worry, dear. It's not as bad as it seems. You two will have this sorted in no time.

"No problem, Mum. We're on it."

Maylie sat on the floor beside Rana. She looked around. She wanted to write there but sitting in the room with Rana was the next best thing.

Rana's mom smiled. "When you're done it'll be time for a special lunch. What do you say?"

"Definitely!" Maylie and Rana exclaimed in unison, and they got to work–Rana stacking papers and Maylie arranging them in bins. After about an hour or so, their task was complete.

Rana ran to get her mom–*or mum*–as she said. Maylie smiled as she put the last programs away and thought of what her mom would say if she called her *mum* when she got back and thinking of her mom's reaction amused her.

She sat on the sofa and glanced over the empty floor. The job had seemed harder when she'd walked in, but it wasn't after all. She was glad to help with official castle business. As long as it didn't have anything to do with the maze, she was fine.

Rana rushed back in and half dragged Maylie out the door. "Come on! You won't believe it."

Maylie kept a firm hand on her bag while they ran. Rana led her out of the castle and toward the grassy area facing the castle across the moat. They made their way down the hill, and Maylie spotted a blanket spread out ahead of them with plates, cups, and a basket on it.

Maylie and Rana looked at each other and squealed.

A picnic.

And, boy, was it a spread–ham and turkey sandwiches cut in little triangles, grapes and strawberries, and two kinds of potato chips–well, *crisps* are what Rana called them.

And while they ate, Rana read the story. She popped grapes in her mouth as she stared at each page. Maylie threw bits of bread to the swans. She tried not to think of the story.

After a few minutes, Rana put the notebook down. "Brill, completely brill, Maylie. I should've had my brother eaten by monsters years ago!"

Maylie had just put a grape in her mouth. She

spit it out like an exploding volcano and snorted with laughter.

Rana joined in until they were both laying on the blanket holding their sides as the sun shone down, and the swans honked loudly as if they were laughing too.

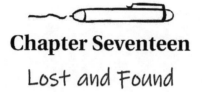

Chapter Seventeen
Lost and Found

Maylie and Rana recovered from the lunch laugh attack and headed back to the castle to help with more concert preparations.

This time they joined Camden and Ravi at one of the booths to sort glow sticks and other "glow gear" as Camden called it.

Packages of glow necklaces and bracelets, crowns and swords, and much more in a wide variety of colors filled dozens of buckets. They separated them by color. Maylie and Rana had their eye on the crowns while Camden and Ravi wanted swords.

Maylie picked up a green sword. "I'll get a crown *and* a sword. Then, I can be a warrior queen."

Camden snorted. "No way. There isn't such a thing as a warrior queen."

Maylie gasped. "There is too."

Camden shrugged.

She walked right up to him and poked him in the stomach with the sword.

"The first Queen Elizabeth was a warrior queen. My guidebook says she even wore armor to speak to her troops before battle."

Maylie folded her arms and pursed her lips. *That should show him.*

Camden threw a skeptical glance at Ravi. "Is that true?"

Ravi gave a slight nod.

"Oh, whatever you say, your Highness." He rolled his eyes and walked past her. "Come on, Ravi. Let's go watch the guys set up the fireworks. That's much more interesting than a history lesson from my sister."

Maylie narrowed her eyes as they walked away. She remembered why they'd written the story in the first place, and she wasn't afraid of it anymore.

"Don't listen to him, Maylie." Rana held up a pink sword. "We can certainly be warrior queens."

Maylie tapped hers against it. "Warrior queens, *break*," she said with a giggle and put the

195

sword back in a bucket. "We'll come back for these later."

Rana gave her a high five. "Now, let's go get my rucksack and your bag from Mum's office."

Rucksack, backpack . . . Rana and her words. Maylie smiled. She was getting the hang of British things and starting to like them. She couldn't wait to teach them to Sarah.

The concert would start in a few hours. Grandma Suey would take her and Camden back to the B&B for an early dinner, and then they'd return for the show.

Rana told her all about the beautiful music that the orchestra would play with their violins, flutes, and many other instruments. She'd never been to a concert like this one before.

At the office, Maylie picked up her bag. Something felt strange about it though. She opened it and sorted through its contents.

Her hand froze. She felt like she'd been punched in the stomach.

Her notebook *wasn't* there.

Maylie began to frantically search the office. She looked under the desk and chair.

"What are you doing?" Rana asked with a frown.

She grabbed Rana's arm. "The notebook isn't in my bag."

Rana gasped and put a hand over her mouth. They both searched the room but didn't find it. They went outside and looked at their picnic spot.

Where was it? Maylie thought so hard her head began to hurt. She was positive that she'd put it back in her bag.

She heard her name called out. She spotted Grandma Suey waving at her from down the walkway. Her head fell to her chest.

Her first story was gone.

Rana walked with Maylie toward Grandma Suey. "Don't worry." Rana put a hand on Maylie's shoulder. "It'll turn up. I'll keep looking, and I'll ask Mum about it."

Maylie nodded. "Thank you. I'll see you soon."

Rana offered a bright smile, but it didn't lift Maylie's spirits nor did dinner. Camden was more annoying than usual, or maybe it was just that Maylie was still mad at him for how he behaved toward her at the glow gear stand.

Grandma Suey asked why Maylie seemed upset, and she told her on the way back to the castle.

"Ah, Maylie, that's awful," she said with a grandmotherly pat on the back. "But like Rana said, 'It'll turn up.'"

Maylie shrugged. She had a bad feeling it was lost forever. That feeling grew when she saw Rana and discovered she nor her mom had seen it.

"Try not to look so glum," Rana said and put an arm around Maylie. "Let's go for those glow crowns and swords."

Maylie gave a small smile. She did want the glow gear.

A few minutes later, Maylie selected a purple crown and blue sword while Rana chose a pink crown and green sword.

For the moment, the lost notebook was forgotten.

Rana led her and Grandma Suey to where Aunt Layla sat at the base of the hill on a blanket sorting through her camera equipment. Maylie sat beside her aunt and watched her arrange long and short lenses inside a bag.

"Hey May." Aunt Layla gave her a hug and looked approvingly at her crown and sword with lights visibly blinking even in daylight. "You're a glowing warrior queen."

Maylie's smile was as bright as the glow gear. "Thanks! That was the idea."

Aunt Layla laughed and stood. "I'm off to work. Enjoy the concert."

Maylie watched Aunt Layla disappear into the massive crowd of people in front of the huge stage far in front of them.

To Maylie, the stage looked like the covered half of a jungle gym its shape was so strange. Two giant TV screens were set up on each side of it, and the castle stood off in the distance.

People filled up the whole grassy area quickly with folding canvas chairs and blankets. Many of them held up small flags of red, white, and blue. Maylie thought of her own country's flag of the same colors. This one had a large "X" in the middle. She pointed it out to Rana. "England's flag, right?"

Rana shook her head. "There is part of England's flag in the design, but it is the United Kingdom's flag. England is this country, but the countries that make up the U.K. are also Scotland, Wales, and Northern Ireland. They are represented within the Union Jack. That's what the flag is called."

"I see," Maylie said. She recognized it from her guidebook. She looked at the flag and admired the design and how it represented several countries. "I guess in a way it's like how our flag represents our states and our country's beginning."

"I'm well aware of the story," Rana said with a smirk. "You, *Yanks*, didn't want us telling you what to do, so you rebelled. There was a lot of terrible things that happened, but the part I actually like is when the people dumped tea into a harbor."

Maylie stifled a giggle with her hand. "I've always liked that part too. I like to imagine giant tea bags floating around in the water."

Rana laughed.

Maylie's expression grew serious. "You know, Rana. If we had lived back then, we couldn't have been friends. We would have been enemies, and that's sad."

Rana smiled and grabbed Maylie's hand. "That may be true. But it was a long time ago, and I think America is all right."

She stood up and pulled a little Union Jack flag from her bag. "In fact, I think we should act as proper representatives of our countries." She handed Maylie the flag. "I'll give this flag to you. And when you return home, you can send one of yours to me. Then, we'll both pretend to be ambassadors for each other's country."

"That's a great idea. I'll start representing right now." Maylie took the flag and waved it wildly over her head.

Rana giggled and shook her head. "Easy now."

Camden and Ravi showed up then with their glowing red swords. Maylie glared back at Camden when he smirked at her like he knew something she didn't.

Grandma Suey headed off the possible confrontation by having Camden and Ravi sit on one side of her and Maylie and Rana sit on the other. Maylie was about to whisper to Rana when someone started talking over the microphone to start the concert.

Their attention went to the stage, and the first musical acts, which Rana said were local singing groups. The singers were good, but Maylie's focus was on the beautiful sunset like a great flaming fire among the clouds above and behind the castle. It was by far the prettiest sight she'd ever seen.

She was so intent on its bright oranges, reds, and golds that she barely heard her name called out by Rana and then something hit her in the back of the head.

"Hey!" She jerked her head right to glare at her brother since she was sure he'd thrown something at her.

But it wasn't her brother.

Rana pointed at a giant inflated beach ball. Maylie burst out laughing and hit the ball back up the hill when it came their way again. In fact, dozens of beach balls bounced up from hands all throughout the crowd. They were *everywhere.*

Camden and Ravi challenged her and Rana to see how many they could hit. Grandma Suey

203

allowed it and kept score as long as they didn't hit anyone.

The music changed from groups of singers to a woman who sang opera in another language and a man who Grandma Suey said sang like an old American singer called Frank Sinatra.

Maylie hit the ball so many times her hand stung, but she was determined not to lose for their team.

The beach balls were put up after a while though, and Grandma announced that the boys had won by two.

Maylie and Rana groaned as Camden and Ravi stuck their tongues out at them.

Grandma caught them though and turned to wag a finger at them when something flew through the air and hit her right smack in the head.

Everyone's mouths dropped clear to the ground. Grandma Suey picked up the object in disbelief. It was a chicken, a rubber chicken.

"If that don't beat all . . ." She held it up by its feet. Then, all five of them started laughing so loud Grandma Suey had to shush them from bothering the people around them.

Grandma Suey called their attention to a plane that flew high above the crowd.

Camden and Ravi pointed excitedly.

"That's a Spitfire plane from the Second World War," Ravi said. "Dad said his grandad flew one in the war. I bet it probably gunned down hundreds of planes to defend Jolly Old England."

The plane zoomed past and then up *high, high, high* into the clouds as it twisted and dove back down and did it again as the orchestra played.

After the airplane disappeared, the music switched to something Maylie and Camden recognized right away as the "Star Wars" theme song. She and Rana conducted with their swords.

When the song finished, Rana said she needed to go to the loo, so Grandma Suey told the boys and Maylie to come along, and they could buy snacks. No one objected, so there they went through the crowd to the vendor booths and bathrooms.

Grandma Suey sat on a bench near the bathrooms. Maylie told Rana that she would go to the glow stand and buy enough glow bracelets to make a huge circle that would stretch around their whole blanket. Rana gave her a high five.

Grandma Suey gave Maylie the money for the glowsticks, and Camden and Ravi stood in line to get food.

The line was long for the glow booth, and when she finally got to the front, she carefully picked an equal number of all colors for their super glow rope. She walked back to Grandma Suey, but Rana wasn't back yet.

"Maylie, would you check on Rana please?" Grandma Suey asked after Maylie handed her the change. "I need to stay here for when the boys come back."

Maylie nodded and headed for the bathroom. She was almost there when Camden ran up to her, his face pale, and eyes wide.

He grabbed her arm and talked in a rushed,

breathless voice, "*Rana, Rana.* We have to stop her!"

Maylie jerked her arm from his grip and held up her hands. "Whoa, whoa, whoa! What are you talking about? Where's Rana?"

He gulped air and grabbed her shoulders this time. "She ran off after I told her where I hid your notebook."

Maylie gasped.

Hid her notebook? He was in BIG trouble!

But she forgot about that. She had to think of her friend first. She grabbed him now and got close to his face. "Where is Rana? Tell me now, Cam!"

"She's gone." He sniffed and stepped back. "She's gone to the maze."

The maze. *No, it couldn't be the maze . . .*

Tears welled in Camden's eyes. He was more scared than Maylie had ever seen him. "Maylie, I–I'm sorry. I'm so sorry! Let's get Grandma Suey and Aunt Layla. They can help find Rana."

Maylie bit her lip to stop from yelling at him. Instead, she pushed past him and ran in the direction of the maze, dodging the huge crowd of people.

She had to save Rana!

Chapter Eighteen
Stories Alive!

Maylie ran along the dimly lit pathway past the castle's gatehouse, the restaurant, museum, and a garden until she saw the maze looming ahead. She stopped and hunched over with hands on her knees trying to catch her breath.

The maze. Maybe she could stop Rana before she went in there alone.

She took off at a full sprint until she reached the entrance. Her feet slipped on the slick grass.

She didn't stop until she stood face to face with the closed metal gate.

Her stomach twisted. A sickening feeling rose into her throat as she tried to steady her breath and look through the bars into the maze as moonlight shone down onto its hedges.

An eerie sensation rushed over her. It was like her story, *just* like her story. She swallowed. Her breaths came too fast. She blinked, unsure if she'd seen a creature slip around a corner dragging a net, or if it was only her imagination.

She shook her head quickly. The motion made her dizzy. No, she didn't have to go in this way. It wasn't like her story. Rana hadn't been here. The gate was locked. She nearly breathed a sigh of relief.

Then, it hit her, and a grip of panic surged through her chest. There were only two ways in and out of the maze. If Rana hadn't been there was she somewhere else?

Maylie forced her feet to move though they felt heavy as bricks. Her heart pounded with each step across the grass and around the metal railing to stand at the very top of a dark set of stairs leading *down, down, down* to the grotto. She shivered from head to toe.

The monster's lair.

Maylie fought to calm the rising panic. Her heart sped up until she could hear a pulse in her throat. The gate to the grotto was open.

Rana.

She took a deep breath and let it out slowly. She couldn't go into the *extreme zone* now. *No, no, no* . . . Her fists tightened, and plastic crinkled against her palm.

The glowsticks.

Maylie hurriedly opened all the packages and cracked them until she held a glowing rainbow in her left hand and her sword in her right.

Warrior queen. That's what she had to be. Rana needed her.

If she didn't see her in the grotto, she would climb to the top of the tower and call out for her. She had to find her.

Maylie had to be braver than ever before. She pushed away the thoughts of the monsters she'd given a home in her imagination and pictured Rana's face. She rushed forward with a yell and held her sword in front of her.

Standing at the bottom, her eyes focused forward into the pitch blackness of the long, winding grotto tunnel. She held the sword out and took a step forward and then another until the blackness swallowed her.

Her hand shook, and a glowstick fell from it like a pink twig onto the tunnel floor. It gave her an idea. She would leave a trail of glowsticks to lead her out after she found Rana.

Maylie inched forward a few steps and dropped a blue one. Her head jerked up when the sound of dripping water reached her ears. The image of the Guardian of the Grotto with glowing red eyes and water pouring from his mouth came to mind. She forced it out.

She swallowed and moved three more steps. Dropping a green stick, she didn't dare look behind her. She moved forward again and dropped a purple one.

Something darted in front of her face, and she nearly screamed. She swung her sword in front of her. A buzzing sounded at her ear. It was only a little bug. She swung her hand this time and shooed it away. She took another breath.

The tunnel stretched on ahead seemingly longer than it had been before. She stopped and listened in case she could hear Rana.

Her hand reached out to the nearest wall. The rough stone scratched her knuckles. Something wet dripped on her hand. The liquid slid down her arm like an icy wet finger.

Maylie tugged her hand to her chest and shivered. She wiped it off on her T-shirt and then dropped a blue glowstick. She pushed forward. She could not let her imagination get the best of her. It was *her* imagination.

With a yell, Maylie crouched low and held her sword forward and charged, dropping a glowstick every few feet toward the end of the tunnel where

216

more stairs led up to the home of the Guardian and the Stone Maidens. She froze suddenly at the end of the tunnel.

She threw a glowstick ahead on the stairs. She did not want to go up those stairs, but she had to go and quickly. She visualized the room–the stone statues in wall cutouts on the left and the great face before her with the stairs leading up on the left.

Before she could talk herself out of it, she yelled, "I'm brave!" and with a surge of courage, she rushed up the stairs with sword drawn and ran straight for the staircase, turning only to throw several glowsticks into the room.

She ran *up, up, up* until she burst out of the grotto into the moonlit maze.

217

She didn't stop for breath but sprinted forward and then up the spiral staircase not allowing herself to even think she'd seen a Stone Maiden in front of her. She ran until she was at the top.

Leaning heavily over the stone wall, she looked down over the huge maze. She spun

around in a circle but didn't see anyone or anything.

Her ears filled with the orchestra's music off in the distance. There was barely any light left in the sky with only the moon above her.

She leaned over the wall and screamed Rana's name just as fireworks exploded and drowned out her voice.

There was no use to scream again.

The fireworks would continue without stopping as Rana said. Maylie tapped her sword's blade against her forehead.

Think, Maylie, think! What should I do?

She looked out across the maze again. She squinted in hope to see Rana somewhere. She glared down at the path that led to the tower.

There was something on the ground.

Maylie rushed down the stairs without a second thought and kneeled to pick up a pink jacket.

Rana's jacket.

The jacket clutched in one hand and her sword still in the other Maylie charged straight into the maze and dared any creature of her imagination to come after her now.

She ran and turned left and then right not slowing or stopping. She ran until she spotted a flashlight on the ground with a huge crack through the plastic. *Rana.*

Up ahead, Maylie thought she heard a shuffling, crunching sound in between fireworks exploding overhead. She froze like Camden and Ravi had in the story. Something was there.

With sword in front of her, she charged again ready to strike whatever was ahead.

When she rounded the corner, she stopped dead in her tracks and dropped the sword. Rana lay up ahead on the ground holding her ankle and crying.

Maylie rushed to her side. "Rana, *Rana*! Are

you okay?"

Rana's eyes widened and then a look of relief passed over her face. "Maylie!" She threw her arms around Maylie's neck and held tight. Definitely as tight as an anaconda.

Maylie pulled back from her grip but didn't let go of her. "Rana, what happened to you? I was so scared."

Rana sniffed a few times until she stopped crying. "I–I went straight to where I knew the maze keys were, grabbed a torch, and came here. I was so angry with our brothers. I barely made it through the grotto." Maylie nodded. "I looked everywhere. I thought I heard something and started running. Then, I tripped and hurt my ankle."

Maylie sat beside Rana. She'd shaken with anger when her brother had told her, and she'd run away. She told Rana everything even the part about the glowstick trail. "I barely made it through the grotto too."

Rana raised her eyebrows. "The story?"

"Yeah, the story," Maylie said and leaned over to examine Rana's ankle. "I can't really see anything." She draped Rana's jacket over her shoulders. "I found your jacket below the tower."

"It was tied to my waist and must have fallen when I ran."

Maylie nodded. "Do you think you can stand up?"

Rana moved her leg, cried out, and then held it still again. "No, Maylie, I can't. It hurts too much."

Maylie frowned. She had to get Rana out of there, but Rana couldn't move. "Rana, you have to get up. We have to at least make it to the tower. You can lean on me."

"No, Maylie. I–I don't think I can."

Maylie leaned down. "Okay, well, I have to go

get help then."

Rana grabbed her arm. "Don't leave me!" Her eyes were so wide and scared. "I'll try to move with your help."

"Okay, Rana. We'll go slow." She helped her friend up and put an arm around her. They carefully moved back through the maze with Rana hopping on one foot while Maylie supported her. They finally reached the stairs and plopped down.

"Ma–Maylie . . . I've been so frightened. I kept thinking I heard or saw things from our story. I was certain a Stone Maiden would snatch me."

Maylie nodded. She understood. But she had to keep Rana distracted until she could think of what to do to get help.

The fireworks.

"Rana, see if you can turn a little bit and put your back to the wall." She winced but did it. "Okay, good. Now, sit here with me and pretend we are sitting on the blanket at the concert and watching the show." Rana raised an eyebrow.

"*Pretend,* Rana. You can do it. I know you can."

Rana swallowed and looked up as the great bursts of red, then white, then blue ignited the sky.

Maylie squeezed her friend's shoulder and looked up too. She had to pretend with her until all she could think about was that Rana was right. The fireworks show was unlike any she had seen.

In the next moment, an explosion of color lit the sky in dozens of continuous bursts.

"The big finale," Rana whispered to Maylie.

Maylie squeezed her shoulder again and forgot about where they were.

The pops of color began to slow with pauses of silence between them, and Maylie thought she heard something else–a muffled yelling.

She shook from Rana's grasp and stood quickly. Her head swam. Her gaze darted left and right. Where was the sound coming from?

Then, two dark shapes emerged from the grotto, and she tensed. *Stone Maidens.*

"Maylie, Rana!" the shapes called out.

She blew out a loud breath as Aunt Layla emerged from the shadows followed by Rana's mom.

Maylie ran as fast as she could and sailed into her aunt's arms. She closed her eyes. They were rescued. Her aunt put her down, and they went to Rana.

Rana's mom wore an expression of relief and anger. "Rana Claire, what were you thinking? You almost killed your dear mum. Don't ever do anything of the sort again." Then, her mom choked up and hugged her.

Her voice softened, "I'm so glad you're okay, love. Let's see about the ankle."

She and Aunt Layla examined it. Maylie could see it was a little puffy and blue. "It looks like a sprain," Aunt Layla said. "We need to put ice on it."

Rana's mom nodded and helped Rana to stand. Her face squeezed in pain at first, but she leaned on her mom's shoulder and started to hop.

Aunt Layla grabbed Maylie's hand, and they were all led out of the maze and grotto following a rainbow trail of glow sticks.

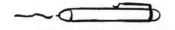

Chapter Nineteen
An Unforgettable Farewell

Maylie sat by Camden on the bed. Neither of them looked at the other. Aunt Layla and Grandma Suey stood in the corner with heads together and voices low. They held her notebook between them.

Maylie wiped tears from her eyes. Her story had caused a huge mess. And Camden hadn't hidden it in the maze after all. It had been in his backpack the whole time. He'd confessed that he had stolen it from her bag.

Maylie and Camden spilled their side of the story with Camden mad at Maylie for writing a terrible story about him, and Maylie mad at Camden for stealing her notebook and tricking Rana into the maze.

But Maylie knew it was both of their faults. She sighed and swallowed the huge lump in her throat.

Her adventure in Europe would be over before it barely began, and she and Camden both knew it.

Mom and Dad had said as much. If they caused *any* trouble, they'd be on the first flight home and would be grounded.

Maylie snuck a peek at her brother. He bit his lip, and she could see he fought back tears too. He didn't want to go home after all. But they had broken the rules.

Rana had gotten hurt. As much as Maylie didn't want to admit it their fighting had gotten out of hand. They deserved whatever was coming.

228

She'd wanted to prove to Aunt Layla, Grandma Suey, and Camden that she was grown-up and responsible. She had blown it big time.

Aunt Layla and Grandma Suey broke from their huddle and paced around the room a minute before facing the bed. "Maylie, Cam . . ." their aunt said in a solemn voice. They both looked up, and Maylie cringed at the look of disappointment on her face.

Aunt Layla cleared her throat and started over again.

"Maylie, Camden–I don't have to tell you how disappointed I am."

She put her hands on her hips. "You are equally responsible. Camden, you shouldn't have teased and annoyed your sister plus stole her notebook and lied about hiding it in the maze. And, Maylie, you shouldn't have used your writing as revenge on your brother and rushed off to the maze without telling an adult what happened first."

Their aunt took a deep breath.

"Rana could've been hurt much worse. I shudder to think what else could have happened." Aunt Layla whirled around, her back to them, and rubbed her forehead. She turned, and her face softened a little. "Do you have anything to say for yourself? To each other?"

Maylie looked at her feet. She knew she needed to apologize to Camden, but part of her couldn't bring herself to do it. She glanced at her aunt and wiped a tear from her cheek.

"Aunt Layla, Grandma Suey, I am so sorry about everything. I let you both down. I should've never tried to get revenge. I'm sorry."

She opened her mouth to say something to Camden, but he spoke up first, his voice quiet. "I'm really sorry too. I shouldn't have done what I did." He paused and turned to Maylie. "I'm really sorry, Maylie."

Maylie raised her head and looked him in the eyes. He meant it. Her brother *really* meant it.

She coughed. "Cam, I–I'm sorry too. I shouldn't have written that story about you and Ravi. And I shouldn't have pushed you and stormed off. Will you forgive me?"

"Yes. Do you forgive me?"

Maylie nodded, and then she looked up at their aunt. "I'm sorry we messed up your job here. You invited us on this trip of a lifetime, and on your first job we messed it up. I don't blame you if you send us home."

Camden nodded.

Aunt Layla squeezed in between them on the bed. She let out a sigh. "You didn't mess up my job. I got the photos I needed, but you did almost give me a heart attack. I've never run so fast in my life."

She put her arms around them. "Okay, here's the deal. Because, and only because, you've apologized and been sincere about it I won't send you home–" Maylie and Camden's heads shot up. "–*yet*."

She looked at Camden and then Maylie. "But if there are *any*, and I mean *any* more problems I will have to send you home. Understand?"

Maylie and Camden bobbed their heads up and down like the swans snatching bread out of the Great Water.

"I love you both so much, and I'm very happy you're with me this summer. I just need to be able to count on you, okay?"

Maylie and Camden hugged her. "All right. Let's get packing. We head back to London tomorrow."

Maylie looked at Camden and smiled.

He smiled back.

Did she still think he was annoying?

Yeah.

But could they be nicer to each other?

Sure.

Grandma Suey came over and held out her notebook. "Maylie, I'd say you've certainly got this writing thing down. But, no more stories of revenge, okay?"

Maylie saluted and said, "Aye, aye, captain!" like the pirates did to Captain Hook in the book.

Grandma Suey laughed and hugged her. Maylie tucked the notebook safely into her bag. From now on she would be much more careful how she used her imagination.

Just like Dr. M had said she had let it run away with her. She shivered. No more maze monsters for her.

The next morning, Maylie rolled her suitcase out

of the B&B and followed Aunt Layla, Grandma Suey, and Camden past the castle toward the main entrance and its castle gift shop—their final stop before leaving for London.

She had a promise to keep.

After shopping for a while, Maylie ended up at the counter with a few postcards, a little replica of the castle, a magnet for Mom and Dad, and a small stuffed swan for Jayna. She proudly scooped up her Leeds Castle shopping bag and walked outside.

"Maylie!" She turned and saw Rana coming toward her on crutches.

Maylie's face fell. Was her ankle broken?

Rana saw her face and smiled. "I'm fine. I'm only using these until the sprain heals. No worries."

Maylie still felt badly about what happened. She told Rana as much.

"It's all right, Maylie. I'm fine. I promise." She pointed a crutch at the bench. "Let's sit."

Maylie helped her to the bench. Rana stretched out her leg, and Maylie could tell her ankle wasn't as puffy. She blew out a breath. "I was so worried about you. I'm sorry about it all."

Rana grabbed her hand. "I know, but despite my injury, I've had a smashing time with you. I will never forget the past few days. Not ever."

"I won't either. Who knew a story could get us into so much trouble?"

Rana nodded with wide eyes. "We'll have to be more careful in the future. Deal?" She held out her hand.

Maylie shook it. "Deal."

"Oh, I nearly forgot." Rana reached into her backpack and pulled out two pens. She handed one to Maylie. It had Leeds Castle and a swan on it. "This is our official pen for *The Pennies.* We can write our stories with it and think of each other."

"Of course!" Maylie exclaimed with a wide smile. "We can type up and send our stories back and forth for our club."

"Yes," Rana said and held up her iPod. "We can text every day!"

Maylie stared at Rana. Her heart felt like it would burst with happiness and at the same time burst from sadness. "Rana, I'll miss you so much." She threw her arms around her.

Rana squeezed tight. "I'll miss you so much too." She pulled back and took both of Maylie's hands in hers. "But we'll stay in touch, and we'll always have *The Pennies*."

"Right-o, Gov'nor!" Maylie said in her best attempt at a Cockney accent.

Rana threw back her head and laughed loudly until she snorted. "Where–" She got out between giggles. "Where did you hear that?"

"In London. Our bus driver who spoke Cockney said it to Cam."

Rana shook her head and pulled the small Union Jack flag from her bag.

"You're now an honorary Brit," she said and handed over the flag like it was a sword. "To a fellow warrior queen of Great Britain. Please take this home as a token of my gratitude for braving the terrifying monsters of the maze to rescue me."

Maylie bowed. "It was an honor." She tucked the flag into her shopping bag. "And I'll be sure to send one to you when I get home."

"Oh, yes, please."

Aunt Layla came up to them. "It's time to go, Maylie." She turned to Rana. "It was nice to meet you. I'm so glad that you two have become such good friends."

"Me too." Rana smiled. She stood, and Maylie hugged her one last time. "I'll write to you soon!"

"You must," Rana said and waved as Maylie

and Aunt Layla walked toward the parking lot. Maylie stopped and looked back. She waved to Rana once more and took a deep breath.

Her first country, castle, and maze. Her first international friend. Her first complete story.

She would not forget a second of her time in England—the good and the bad. And she wouldn't forget her second chance to stay on this amazing adventure.

Aunt Layla put an arm around Maylie. "You ready, May?"

Maylie looked up at her. "Yes, I am."

They turned and walked together to Grandma Suey and Camden, who stood by their suitcases and a taxi ready to take them to the train station and then onto London.

Camden leaned over his suitcase. "Aunt Layla, where are we going next?"

"A magical place—" Aunt Layla's eyes held a mischievous gleam. "—home to leprechauns and pots o' gold at the end of rainbows. *Ireland.*"

"Ireland." A thrill shot through Maylie when she said it aloud.

Camden frowned. "Ireland. So, that's where the Lucky Charms guy is from?"

Aunt Layla laughed and in her best Irish accent said, "I guess so, me boy-o. You'll hafta wait and see."

Everyone burst out laughing, then Maylie pumped her fist in the air.

"Ireland, here we come!"

THE END

Author's Note

The character of Maylie came to my mind like a friend I hadn't seen in a while. It was like, "Oh yeah, Maylie. I need to talk to her soon."

We're a lot alike. We both love to write and have overactive imaginations that tend to run away with us sometimes. We both like new experiences even if we're a bit nervous about them at first, and like Maylie by this book's end I can't wait to travel to my next country!

The maze was the second thing that came to my mind. When I visited Leeds Castle after I graduated college that beautiful place with its intriguing maze stayed with me. The grotto especially made an impression as it certainly did for Maylie. I knew it had to play a big part in this story.

Through this book and the ***Tales of a Travel Girl*** series, I want you, Readers, to have a chance to travel the world through fiction and along the way learn a bit. I've tapped into my own first-hand experiences from traveling to over a dozen countries and filtered a few of them through Maylie's eyes.

Throughout the series we follow Maylie as she chases after her writing dreams. What are YOUR dreams? How are you chasing after them?

No matter what roadblocks stand in your way go for it! Dream BIG! I believe in you!

ACKNOWLEDGMENTS

First of all, THANK YOU, Reader!! Without you Maylie's story wouldn't truly come to life! I hope you enjoyed your journey with Maylie to England. I also hope you'll check out the next book in the series as Maylie travels next to the amazing country of Ireland.

I would like to thank my family and friends for all their support and encouragement of my writing and this book. I couldn't have done this without you! A special thank you to my husband, Steven, and my son, Gareth. Also to my mom, Mellanie; mother-in-law Jennifer; sister Anna and friends, Brooke and Alexis.

Thank you to Sam and Melanie at Leeds Castle for your assistance and kindness and to the Leeds Castle Foundation for permission to print the photographs I took during my visit there.

A HUGE THANK YOU goes out to an amazing group of beta readers. Firstly, being my writing partner and dear friend, Carole Lehr Johnson. Thank you for all you've done and all you do! To my adult beta readers, thank you! – Erin Masters, Jennifer Benandi, Jill Nadler (aka Riley Roam), Donna Estis, Ashtin Nugent, Bridget Neace, Jill Reid, Danna Walker, Jen Sharbono, Leann Smith, Stacie Prather, Katie Firmin, Johnnie Alexander, Tracy Joy, and Sara (Helams) Hodges. Thank you to the talented editor, Ellen Brock, whose critique of this book raised tough questions and helped get Maylie's story into shape.

Thank you A MILLION to my kid beta readers – Rylee M., Ceanna B., Caitlyn W., Chloe H., Callum P., Gracie C., Jessica S., Riley S., Sadie S., Callie S., and Ellie R.

To my Word Wanderers group – THANK YOU! Erin, Jennifer B., Tracy, Sam, Cathy, Kaylee, Jennifer S., Mellanie, Reagan, Lizzie, and Katie. Forgive me if I've left anyone out because so many people have graciously helped me with this book!

I can't leave out the AMAZING artist who literally brought Maylie's story to life through her INCREDIBLE illustrations – Monica Bruenjes (www.artistmonica.com).

THANK YOU, THANK YOU, THANK YOU!! I couldn't have a better partner in crime! I've enjoyed every moment of working with you. I can't wait until the next book when we once again stay up too late chatting about book cover fonts, agonizing over Camden's facial expressions, and trying to remember Maylie isn't left-handed.

And I would like to thank God, who formed my creative mind and gave me a heart for stories that shine light in darkness and inspire.

PETER PAN

Peter Pan is a classic children's novel written by author J.M. Barrie from his popular stage play of the same name that was first performed on stage in 1904. The novel's actual name is "Peter and Wendy," though it is known as "Peter Pan." It was published in 1911.

ABOUT THE BOOK

Peter Pan, the boy who won't grow up, meets the Darlings – Wendy, John, and Michael – and convinces them to fly away with him to Neverland where they encounter the Lost Boys, pirates and the despicable Captain Hook.

ABOUT THE AUTHOR

Sir James Matthew Barrie was born on May 9, 1860

in the town of Kirriemuir, Scotland. Barrie was less than five feet tall due to a condition called psychogenic dwarfism linked to childhood trauma over his brother's tragic death. Barrie received higher education and worked as a journalist. He moved to London, and, in 1887, wrote his first novel and a few years later started writing for the theater. His play, "Peter Pan," was a massive success. He died in 1937.

DISCUSSION QUESTIONS

How does reading **Peter Pan** inspire Maylie to embrace her imagination and think impossible things? What part(s) in **Peter Pan** sparked your imagination the most?

Like Wendy wanting to grow up, why does Maylie want to grow up? Are you ready to grow up? If yes, why? If not, what do you enjoy most about being a kid?

In London, Maylie loves seeing the "Big Ben" clock tower because in the animated "Peter Pan" film it is where Peter, Wendy, and her brothers fly past going to Neverland. Have you seen a landmark in real life from a movie or TV show? If yes, what did you think about it?

LEEDS CASTLE

Leeds Castle is such an incredible place and has such a fascinating history. I mean, it's nearly 1,000 years old!! Wow!!

Leeds Castle has been a Norman stronghold, the private property of six of England's medieval queens, a palace used by King Henry VIII, a Jacobean country house, a Georgian mansion, an elegant retreat for the rich and famous, and today, it is one of the most visited historic buildings in Britain.[1]

The first stone castle was built in 1119. In 1278, it was acquired by Queen Eleanor of Castile, the first wife of Edward I.

For the next 300 years the castle remained a royal residence, before again becoming a private home and handed down over four centuries until purchased in 1926 by an American-born heiress.

There's not just a castle but, of course, a hedge maze and over 500 acres of gardens, parkland, and wildlife. There are also a host of activities and attractions including falconry demonstrations, a dog collar museum, zipline and Segway tours, playgrounds, miniature golf, and more.

But now more about the maze.

When the Leeds Castle Maze is viewed from its center, part of its plan mirrors a queen's crown. It is set in a square, and yet, when seen from the mound or the air, the pattern is circular, this is unique to Leeds Castle and adds to the difficulty in solving it.[2]

Me lost in the maze

A maze is filled with dead ends and tends to attract those more interested in solving puzzles and facing challenges. The word "maze" dates from the 13th century and comes from the Middle English word *mæs*, denoting delirium or delusion.[3] In the United States, the most famous mazes–and the largest–are made from corn.[3]

The maze, created in 1988 by the world's leading maze designer Adrian Fisher, is made up of over 2,400 yew trees. It is also the only one to

have even baffled its creator - upon opening it to the public, even he couldn't find his way out.[2]

Today, the attraction is still one of England's most popular and complicated mazes. To exit, you venture through a mysterious underground shell grotto, twisting and turning through a combination of tunnels. For more info, visit www.leeds-castle.com or hopefully visit it in person.

1. Leeds Castle official website, https://www.leeds-castle.com/.

2. "Leeds Castle Maze Turns 30!" Leeds Castle official website, last modified 7 August 2018, https://www.leeds-castle.com/news/Leeds+Castle+News/Leeds+Castle+Maze+Turns+30.

3. "A Brief History of Mazes," National Building Museum, last modified 24 June 2014, https://www.nbm.org/brief-history-mazes/.

4. "The Winding History of the Maze," Smithsonian Magazine, last modified 31 July 2014, https://www.smithsonianmag.com/travel/winding-history-maze-180951998/.

DISCUSSION GUIDE

 Maylie is frustrated that she can't write a single story. When have you been frustrated because you couldn't do something? What did you do?

 Would you feel worried like Maylie about going far from home to another country? Why?

 Maylie has a giant map of the world on her bedroom wall. What country would you love to visit the most and why?

 Camden accuses Maylie of not having fun anymore. Maylie feels like she is too old to act like a kid. Do you feel this way? Does it matter to you like it does to Maylie?

 When Maylie learns that Rana is alone in the maze, she rushes to rescue her friend. Would you do that? Why?

 Maylie knows she needs to apologize to her brother, but it is hard for her to do. Why do you think it is hard to apologize?

Travel with Maylie to Ireland

in Book Two of the
Tales of a Travel Girl series...
Coming Spring 2021!

Turn the page for a preview!

For updates, **SIGN UP** for

Author M.L. Tarpley's newsletter at

www.mltarpleybooks.com

Chapter One

Ships Ahoy

The boat might as well have been the Titanic
because I was doomed.

Swoosh! Maylie whipped off her sunglasses.
Her eyes widened as she stood at the ferry
terminal behind Aunt Layla, Grandma Suey, and
Camden and looked *up, up, up* the levels of the
ship.

Yes, ship, with its large green and orange fin
sporting an Irish flag and "ISE" for Irish Sea
Express in large letters.

"This is the ferry?" she asked, her mouth

hanging open. The boat in front of her was huge!

Aunt Layla whirled. Her shoulder-length red hair rippled in the sunlight. "Yep. What were you expecting, May?"

Maylie shrugged. She'd never been on a ferry. "This looks more like a cruise ship to me."

Her aunt smiled and waved her hand toward the boat with a dramatic flair. "Then, step right up. Welcome aboard your afternoon cruise on the Irish Sea!" She messed up Cam's hair and elbowed him in the side. "You can swab the poop deck, matie!"

He swatted her arm away playfully. "No way!" He pointed to Maylie. "She can do that."

"Not me!" Maylie said in disgust and crossed her arms. "Besides, this isn't a pirate ship."

"A little imagination won't hurt you, Maylie. We know you have tons of it," he said with a dark glare. She was sure the look meant he still hadn't fully forgiven her for the horror story she'd written about him in England. He shook his head and turned back to Aunt Layla. "Aye, aye, Captain!"

Their aunt laughed and hugged him, and they rushed forward onto the ship.

Maylie raised an eyebrow and sighed. If Cam kept up this childish behavior, he would be sent home for sure. Maylie couldn't take that risk even with Aunt Layla joking around too. She might slip up. She was already on her second chance. She would not be sent home.

Maylie's hand shook as she grabbed the handrail. Usually, she wasn't quite so serious, but she had a secret–a horrible, terrible secret–that no one knew.

She was scared to death of boats.

On the train ride through the country of Wales that morning, she'd even had a pep talk with herself that went something like: *Maylie, it's only a boat ride. As in one. From Wales to Ireland. You can do this.*

According to the map, the distance between the countries was barely the length of two fingernails. She could sit and read the next book her aunt had given her–*The Lion, the Witch and the Wardrobe* by C.S. Lewis, one of the famous writers she'd learned about in her writing class in London.

Her plan was set. Become so lost in the book that the boat ride would be over in a blink.

Her speech fell completely flat now. If the boat was this big, there was absolutely no way that it was only a short ride. She swallowed the lump in her throat. Her head spun until she took a deep breath.

It was *too* late. She was here, and she'd rather squirm than admit her fear.

Maylie popped her sunglasses back on and followed the others onto the ship.

Inside, Camden rubbed his hands together and glanced up at Aunt Layla. "Is there an all-you-can-eat buffet?" He patted his stomach. "Because I could fit two whole pizzas in here."

Aunt Layla threw back her head and laughed. "Well, aren't you just the comedian today, Cam.

You should host your own show. *Comedy with Cam*. And, sorry, but, no, there's not a buffet."

He shrugged and then smiled. Maylie's stomach lurched. She wasn't sure if it was from Camden's praise, or the ship moving slightly under her feet.

The ship.

She looked around her. An endless sea of short, prickly green carpet stretched in all directions. A small white-haired lady, not much taller than Maylie, passed by pulling a shopping bag on wheels. The bag brushing against the carpet made a low, swishing sound like the flutter of book pages.

"Come on, Maylie," Aunt Layla called out ahead of her with a wave. "Let's explore!"

The weird plastic carpet spread outside onto the deck, and Maylie realized it was meant for wet surfaces.

She froze. Maybe for easy clean-up after people got sick?

A sudden dizziness hit her. She stumbled forward and steadied herself against a deck chair.

Grandma Suey reached out to her. "You okay?"

Maylie gripped the chair arm a second and then straightened and nodded. She grasped her bag strap with both hands. "I–I'm fine. I just lost my footing."

"Okay, then. Easy does it." She squeezed Maylie's shoulder. "Let's catch up to the others. Those two are probably scheming up a way to convince the captain to let them steer the ship."

Maylie frowned and walked on. Her bag strap like a life preserver as the ship came alive under her feet, a sleeping giant roaring to life.

Want to learn to write like Maylie did?

SIGN UP for Author M.L. Tarpley's newsletter & receive your own FREE downloadable **Young Writer's Kit!***

PLUS hear about book news, fun activities & crafts, what she's reading & more!

Sign up at www.mltarpleybooks.com

*a print version is also available on Amazon

Q&A with the AUTHOR

M. L. TARPLEY

Why did you choose England for the setting of *Maylie and the Maze*? What is it about this country that interests you?

The book had to be set in England because that's where the maze is located. Plus, I love England! I love the countryside and manor houses and castles and the mix of modern-day and history in the city of London. My favorite place is the city of Bath.

What are your favorite scenes in the book?

That's a hard question. I think it would have to be between the first time Maylie goes into the maze and grotto and when she has to rescue Rana. I love how she uses her glow gear and how brave she has to be to overcome her fear to help her friend.

What are your favorite illustrations in this book?

Artist Monica Bruenjes is very talented! I LOVE them all, but if I have to pick, my absolute favorite is of Maylie, Camden, and Grandma Suey riding on the double decker bus. I have the original print framed to hang on my wall. It brings back memories of my visits to London!

I also love the illustrations outside of Harrod's when Camden bumps into the lady and their lunch by the Peter Pan statue.

What do you hope readers take away from this book?

That you can do anything you set your mind to, AND you can travel anywhere in the world (or fictional ones) from the pages of a book. Happy Travels!!

Please share a favorite memory of your travels in England.

One of my favorite memories is staying a few nights in a 500-year-old thatched cottage in a tiny English village surrounded by green fields edged with low stone fences and full of sheep. "Thatched" means the roof is made of a special straw.

ABOUT THE AUTHOR

M.L. TARPLEY

※ **Author M.L. Tarpley** writes stories of adventure, friendship, and fun that transport kids to amazing places across the world. She is also an award-winning journalist and world traveler.

Besides writing and traveling to over a dozen countries, her other interests include hanging out at cool coffee shops, listening to vintage records, going on adventures with her family, and researching dead people in her family from long ago (*cough* it's called genealogy). She lives in Louisiana with her husband and son.

For more information, check out

www.mltarpleybooks.com

ABOUT THE ARTIST

MONICA BRUENJES

Artist Monica Bruenjes specializes in original animation, comics, and illustration.

She holds a MFA in 3D Animation from the Academy of Art University. She loves to travel and lived in Japan for a year.

She is the creator of the comic book, Penguin & Peep (www.penguinpeep.com).

Originally from California, she now lives with her husband in Wisconsin to be near bears, deer, and the occasional porcupine.

For more information, check out

www.artistmonica.com

Did you enjoy this book?
Would you write a review?

The more reviews, the more chances
other kids can enjoy this book*

WRITING A REVIEW

Keep it simple (to a few sentences)
& include the following:

- **NAME THE TITLE & AUTHOR**
- **WHAT WAS THE BOOK ABOUT?**
  (BE BRIEF. NO SPOILERS.)
- **WHAT DID YOU LIKE ABOUT IT**
  OR NOT LIKE ABOUT IT?
- **WOULD YOU RECOMMEND THIS**
  BOOK TO OTHERS? WHY?

*Please ask an adult to post your book review
on Goodreads, Amazon, and/or
any other seller's website.

Thanks a million!!

Made in the USA
Las Vegas, NV
09 November 2021